Elisabeth Margaretha Countess of Schoengau-Brixendorf
Golden Straw in my Hair

Bibliografische Information
der Deutschen Nationalbibliothek
Die Deutsche Nationalbibliothek verzeichnet diese
Publikation in der Deutschen Nationalbibliografie; detaillierte
bibliografische Daten sind im Internet über
http://dnb.d-nb.de abrufbar.

Herstellung und Verlag:
Books on Demand GmbH Norderstedt
© Elisabeth Margaretha
Countess of Schoengau-Brixendorf 2015
All rights reserved
The works – even parts of it – may only be shared
with the permission of the author.
ISBN 9783734747700

Elisabeth Margaretha
Countess of
Schoengau-Brixendorf

Golden Straw in my Hair

from the series "Strong Ladies"

"Your first book Sara, the weasel made a hit. Do you feel like writing a second one? I have got a super story for you".
My editor was on the phone.
Why not? I had to admit, that I grew to like it. I had him give me some information and set on my way to the North German lowlands right the next weekend. After many talks, the reading of many pages of diary entries and the one or other research I had all the facts I needed. Now it could start.

"Corporal Brandes"!
"Yes, Mr. Sergeant, Sir"?
"Pack your things together. You have got two weeks home leave".
Gerd Brandes didn't hesitate. Pleasantly surprised he got his few belongings ready and contacted the driver. Two full weeks off this shit. Could there be anything better? In his mind he went through the return from the front again and again. Three days home and three days back, if everything went well, he could probably stay full eight days with his loved ones at home.
The convoy of trucks rattled westbound on streets full of holes and eroded open trails, through completely destroyed villages. When they finally reached German areas of the Empire in Pomerania, Gerd Brandes felt something like feeling at home. Here people spoke German. Another one and a half days and he would be able to hug his Helena. He had never seen his daughter Antje yet. Would she recognize him as her father? Well, maybe Helena had shown a photo to the little one.
From Breslau the journey went on by train. Even before they were able to reach Frankfurt/Oder the train had stopped several times. All passengers had to leave the wagons. Gerd had made his way into the next bushes and ducked his head. Only seconds later he heard the infernal rattling of the machine

guns. Russian hunters were attacking the train and hammered one volley after the other into the roofs of the wagons. The gunners immediately targeted everything moving. A few old women ran like hares but had no chance of escaping the attack. When the hunters had retreated and Gerd got out of the bushes he was offered a horrible sight. About fifty people hadn't survived the massacre.
"Listen everybody!"
Gerd strained his ears.
"The women will carry the dead bodies onto a heap over there. Somebody else will take care of the burial. We don't have time for it now. The men will come here to me"!
"Where's the train driver"?
"I'm here, Mr. Standartenfuehrer (high-ranking SS officer)".
"Get onto the engine and check if it is able to drive at once".
The train driver walked away.
"All the other men are going to follow me now".
The standartenfuehrer ran towards one of the wagons in the center.
„It is gone, as you can see. We are going to decouple and overturn it. Come on".
While some of the men started working at the clutches, the officer ran forward to the loco.

"When I say 'Now', you are going to drive a few meters forward, ok"?

The train driver nodded.

"Is everything ready over there"?

"Yes, Mr. Standartenfuehrer, the clutches are disengaged".

The officer gave the train driver a sign and the engine started. After a few meters the officer had him stop and ran back.

„Now you are going to push the wagon two meters forward. It must stand free, not that something happens".

The men pushed and the wagon slowly set in motion.

"Well, that's enough. Now everybody to the left side".

All the men stood next to the wagon.

"To my sign you start lifting. I want the damaged wagon to fall from the tracks. Give it a full bounce. I don't want this old thing to jam the traffic. Come on now".

All the men stood in a line and grasped.

"Now"!

All the men tensed their muscles and the left side of the wagon lifted a few centimeters from the tracks indeed.

"Stop it. It won't work like this".

He let the man stand and ran over to the women who were busy stapling the dead bodies.
"Come over to us. You have to give a helping hand".
The women left the dead bodies and followed the officer to the wagon.
"The women are going to build a dense line exactly in front of the wagon. You and you and you are going to fill up the gaps. You others stand behind the women and grasp past them, ok"?
"Yes, Mr. Standartenfuehrer".
"Attention: now"!
Almost a hundred persons simultaneously lifted up and slowly the wagon lifted out of the tracks on one side.
"Keep on going. Don't lose your touch. Go a few steps forward and then you'll succeed".
Like in slow motion the sloping position of the wagon increased.
"Come on, give it everything"!
Then the death point was overcome and the wagon tilted aside almost on its own.
"Step aside, not that something happens".
Everybody jumped backwards and observed the wagon completely tilting aside.
"Shit, it is too near to the tracks. Train driver, come here"!

The train driver who had helped tilting stood at attention.

"Do you think the engine is strong enough to push the tilted wagon away"?

"Yes, Mr. Standartenfuehrer. It is a real Adler. It will waltz through it".

"Well, then see to it that you get into your engine and drive a few meters backwards onto my sign. Then the first wagons can push aside the tilted one. Did you understand me"?

"Yes, Mr. Standartenfuehrer".

"Come on, come on, take your heater and put some coal onto it. I want to be off here before the Russians come back".

The heater blackened with soot and white streams of sweat in his face and the train driver ran away to enter the engine a few seconds later. After another few seconds the engine slowly started moving backwards. The officer directed the train driver with expansive gestures and centimeter by centimeter the last wagon approached to the wagon lying next to the tracks. Now the buffer on the right hand backside of the rolling wagon touched the arbor of the lying one. A creaking noise was to be heard when the lying wagon was pushed over the rail track ballast. Shortly before the driving wagon was about to jump from the tracks the officer had it stop and waved the train driver to come to him.

"What do you think? Will it be ok"?
"If we manage to couple the wagons at the back again, we'll mange it all".
The officer again turned towards the passengers.
"You and you and you, you uncouple the first of the wagons in the back, come on, hurry up".
The men ran off.
"Ok, Mr. Standartenfuehrer, the wagon is uncoupled".
"Well now everybody, men and women behind the wagon. You push as fast as you can".
Everybody who found a space, stood behind the wagon now.
"You and you stand to the side. You can also push from there. Now, you are going to start on my sign. And give it everything, we have to go on".
The officer took his position and waved. The men pushed the wagon with all their power and set it into motion.
"Push, push, push"!
The wagon gathered speed and crashed against the center line of the lying wagon. There was enough speed to push the lying wagon off the tracks. However the pushed wagon had so much speed, that it loudly crashed into the last wagon of the ones in front. Nothing was damaged because the buffers could easily cushion the impact.

The officer gave the train driver a sign. He had the train roll back slowly. Now all the wagons were in a line again.

"Couple".

"Already done, Mr. Standartenfuehrer".

"Come on, get inside, the hurt ones first".

When everybody was on board again the officer had them get started. Slowly the train set into motion. Gerd Brandes and the others were pleased to get on. More than one hour had passed since the attack. He hoped to reach the connecting train in Berlin.

Hardly thirty minutes later, Gerd Brandes was torn out of his thoughts.

"Papers"!

When he looked up he recognized the standartenfuehrer in front of him.

"Papers, be quick about it".

"What's the matter"?

"I'm the one to ask questions. We want to see whether someone is going to make a getaway".

Gerd Brandes opened his backpack to get out his pay book and furlough.

"Hurry up I don't have much time"!

The two SS men accompanying the officer lifted their machine guns. Gerd Brandes hurried and gave the officer his papers.

"Seems to be alright".

The officer gave Gerd Brandes his papers back and checked the next passenger.

"Here everything blows up into our face and these idiots have nothing else to do but hassle people and babble about the final victory", one of his fellow passengers whispered to him.

He only nodded and emerged into his thoughts again. Why should he get upset about these madmen? He wanted to go home, nothing else counted for him.

Shortly before arriving in Berlin he got the next bad news.

"Berlin is impossible. The tracks are broken. We have to fall back on Lueneburg. Maybe we can reach Hamburg from the South. Who wants to Berlin has to get off at the next station".

While about a third of the passengers left the train at the next station, Gerd Brandes and his comrades were looking for a better seat. A few benches had been damaged at the air attack and he was pleased to be able to sit properly again.

Hours later the train arrived at Lueneburg main station. Two railway officials walked up and down the train.

"Stay seated. We are going to leave for Hamburg in a moment".

When the train passed the suburbs of Hamburg, Gerd realized at once what must have happened.

Entire streets lay in ashes, oh goodness! Hopefully nothing had happened to his family.

"Don't worry. Where you want to go nothing had happened. The Tommies won't throw their bombs onto lonesome fields".

Only late in the evening he reached Bremervoerde. He threw his backpack round his shoulders and marched off. He had survived so many cruelties. Now these few kilometers couldn't really upset him anymore. At about midnight he saw the first houses of Bartelshain. His home village lay peacefully in front of him in the darkness. The tower clock stroke twelve times and heralded the start of a new day. It was the sixth of July in 1944. The fourth birthday of his daughter Antje had just begun.

Some minutes later he reached the farm where he had grown up. Although he was dead tired he kept standing in front of the building for a moment to take the sight in. Although only sparely lit by the moonlight he absorbed each corner, each brick. Then he left his thoughts and pushed the door handle down. The door was unlocked as usual. Silently he slipped through the hall and went upstairs. Helena and Antje were fast asleep.

He approached the bed very slowly to avoid the creaking of the floor boards. He first squatted down and then grasped under the cover. His hands reached the warm soft body of his wife. He caressed her for a few moments. Suddenly she turned round and starred at him in shock. He put a forefinger onto the lips and kissed her. Now she completely turned to him and strongly hugged him.

He slipped and gave her a sign. She nodded when she understood. Silently he slipped out of the bedroom. Helena carefully got up and followed him. At the edge of the stair she hugged him. Now he hugged her as well and tore her towards the kitchen.

"Sorry for seeming to be so unapproachable but I am starving".

Helena smiled and took the lead into the kitchen.

"Are a few slices of bread with mettwurst enough"?

"Whatever! As long as there is good food. I can't see this slop from the front any longer".

Helena nimbly cut a few slices off the loaf, spread a thick layer of butter onto it and put mettwurst slices of a few centimeters onto it. While Gerd greedily bit into his first slice Helena went to get a bottle of beer from the food locker.

"Now tell me, how are you? You don't look too well".

"It is hell. The Iwan is blasting out of all their barrels. We are sitting in the dirt all the time, because the planes don't leave us alone for a second. Whole units have had it. We don't have anything reasonable to eat. Not to talk about the supplies. I ask myself what all this should still be good for. We won't be able to fight the Russians anyway. The officers have given up for long but don't dare to tell it, because everybody is put up against the wall who doesn't believe in the final victory. I've been fed up with it for long. Obviously I'm not born to be a hero".

"Well, I know that. Here are some idiots as well, who have no other topic from morning till night. The other day they even took us two pigs. For the final victory they said. One we had slaughtered illicitly. In Bederkesa they caught one with it and immediately hung him. It would be sabotage and subversion of the war effort they shouted. Nobody dares even to think aloud any more. There are informers everywhere. You won't believe who joined them".

"We have informers in the village"?

"Of course, and Adolf Wilbers from kitty-corner is the worst of them all".

"He's the one to need it. Can't count to ten, but has a big mouth".

"Yes, his son Manfred sits in England".

"He had been caught in France and is certainly better off now than the ones who are stuck in Russia. For him the war is over and if you believe what people tell they don't have a really bad life in England".

"I don't want to fall into the hands of the Russians. They won't treat us well after what we had done on our way to the east. I came through large ruin fields. Dead bodies of humans and animals spread all over. Even from the smallest villages they had left only smoking remains. I tell you, this won't end well for us.

I was even supposed to kill Jews the SS had rounded up. But I said no, I won't do things like that. They didn't do anything to me. I can't be delighted in treating humans like cattle and simply shooting them down as a few others are able to. They get into a really dizzied state, when they are able to torture or slaughter these poor people. They even have fun and mock, laugh and smirk when the skirt of a Jewish woman blows up. I don't even want to know what the matter is in the camps after all. I can well imagine things like that with Adolf Wilbers, too. When he is alone he shits a brick. But you better not meet him when his mates are with him. Then woe may betide you"!

"When do you have to leave again"?

"In a week, I'll rather start a day earlier. You never know what will happen on the way. I don't want to be late. In the meantime they hang everybody they count for a coward or renegade".

At about three in the morning they both fell asleep closely huddled against each other.

As most of the men had been conscripted, on the small farms a lot of work had been left behind. Helena tried her best to keep house and farm in order and to till the fields but had reached her limits long time ago. Although neighbors had helped now and then, there had only been time for the most necessary.

Right the next morning Gerd Brandes visited his friends in the village. He talked a neighbor into giving him the wooden doll of her adult daughter and joyfully gave it to Antje as a birthday present. Other celebrations had to be cancelled and delayed to the time after the final victory.

Gerd was hardly back on his farm, when he and his wife packed a few rakes and a scythe onto a small cart, harnessed the only left horse and went to the near meadow where the grass had been waiting for a cut for weeks. Gerd immediately started mowing and Elena spread a blanket. They had left without a breakfast and this had to be made up for now.

After Gerd had mowed about half of the meadow, they ate the bread and sausage they had brought with them. Only ten minutes later Gerd swung the scythe again. After Helena had packed away the blanket, she started to ted the freshly cut grass of the first half with the rake. In the meantime Antje joyfully jumped around the field and again and again gave her new doll a squeeze.

Suddenly Gerd let his scythe fall down and approached Helena. He took away her rake and hugged her. Immediately Antje came jumping and was included into the hugging as a matter of course.
„Hopefully this bullshit is over soon. Sometimes I am craving for you when I am lying in the Russian dirt. Sometimes I am scared to death and think of you deliberately in order to not go insane".
Helena didn't answer. She just enjoyed the nearness of her husband.
After Gerd had shortened the last blade of grass, they both made a break. In greedy gulps they had the tea run down their throats, which Elena had cooked while Gerd had been in the village.
"Come on, another round of turning hay and then let's go home. I must admit I'm not used to this work anymore after so many months".
Although Gerd gave his best, he didn't succeed of course to do all the overdue work in his short time of furlough. The days had passed in a flash and the day of his farewell had come. After a last tender night with Helena he started off early in the morning.
"Come back safe and sound".
"Of course I'll come back. I can't leave my beautiful Helena alone".

"Don't talk such a fuss. The beauty has gone for long. Now an old worked out woman stands before you".

"What are you talking? You are the most beautiful woman of the world and the real Helena from Troy would go green with envy, if she could see you now".

"You are a real nut"

Antje was still fast asleep when after a last hug he left the house and set for his way to Bremervoerde to return to his troops.

*

Although he actually had started one day too early he hardly managed to reach his troop in time. The train had had to stop again and again. People were shot down again and again. Several times he had to change the train, because locos, wagons and whole tracks had been destroyed.

"Brandes, man, where in the world are you? There is utter chaos here".

"Why? I have come in time. My furlough is actually until this evening".

"No speechifying. Come on, come on, the final victory is waiting".

The sergeant had uttered his last words with a twinkling eye and much too loudly. Gerd knew at once what he meant. There must be a gestapo or SS spy around here again. Those spies saw to it that even the greatest doubters believed in the final victory again at once.

Basically nothing had changed at the front, except for having gone a few kilometers westward. 'Orderly retreat' and 'straitening of the front' the propaganda boastfully called it. If they had asked the common soldiers for their opinion, they would have packed their bundle for long and would have gone home. But neither Gerd Brandes nor any other had been asked for their opinion.

The truth of the matter is that Gerd could be happy to be still alive. After those horrible battles in icy winter, after the slaughters in knee-deep mud, after the permanent massive attacks of the Russians, their rows were strongly decimated. He wasn't able to count anymore how many comrades he had had to leave back in the mud. Some had been just shot nest to him. Others had been completely torn to pieces. Parts of bodies had flown through the air. Men without head had walked on a few meters. Men without limbs had still screamed for a few minutes before they faded away. Bullets and shell splinters had blown up in his face. He would never forget this high piping and buzzing, those screams, this ear deafening hammering of the machine guns.

On the fourth day after his furlough a SS-man approached him.

"Brandes, I heard that a few months ago you denied shooting down a few fucking Jews. Is that true?"

"Yes, I'm not a good shooter".

"Excuses, nothing but excuses! Admit it, you liked these Jewish broads".

"That is not true".

"Follow me".

With a foreboding of evil Gerd Brandes followed him at once. You better don't mess with people like this.

After a few minutes they reached a small wood or better what had been left of it. There was hardly any green, only dead trunks rose up to the sky here and there. They had tied men onto two of these trunks.

"Now Brandes, you can patch things up again".

"What am I supposed to do"?

"These are deserters. They cowardly wanted to get away. You know what will be done to deserters, do you"?

"They are brought to a war court".

"Nonsense! Do you see a war courts anywhere here? You are going to shoot them down, ok"?

"But we can't just shoot them down. They must be brought to a war court first".

"Shut up. I am the war court here, if you insist of having one. And the war court has just decided these two deserters have to be shot down. Have you understood it"?

"You can tell me what you want to. You are not empowered to act as a war court here. These men must be brought to an ordinary war court".

"Well Brandes, have you become courageous at once? These are deserters and you are going to shoot them and that's the end of the discussion"

"No, these men have to be brought to an ordinary war court. And that's why I won't shoot them down".

The gun stock hit Gerd completely unprepared. He felt his jawbone breaking. He shortly staggered. Then his legs gave way. In times past he had thought such a hit must pain. No, nothing pained. His head roared. His mouth had gone numb, but he didn't feel any pains. He turned his head aside and saw the SS-man shooting down the alleged deserters. Then the man turned to him, smiled wryly and pulled the trigger. Gerd looked astonished at the SS-man.

*

In the same moment when the heartbeat of Gerd finally ceased, his daughter Antje a few houses further was happily playing with the one year older neighbor boy Guenter, his brother Uwe and sister Mathilde while Helena brought the hay from the meadow with the help of two neighbor women.

*

The SS-man, as cool as ice, cut the dead men from the tree and cleared away. The dead bodies had been found a few hours later and were buried in a mass grave. Nobody doubted that these three men had been killed by a Russian volley.

*

Three weeks later Adolf Hilbert suddenly stood in front of Helena's door.
"I'm really sorry but I have to tell you that your Gerd was bravely killed in action for fuehrer, nation and fatherland. Here's the letter of his major".
Helena looked at the man in surprise.

"This can't be true. He promised me to come back. This must be an error. Admit that you want to do a bad joke with me".

"I don't do any jokes on things like that".

Helena took the letter from his hands, opened the envelope and started reading. Suddenly the lines faded from her eyes. She let her fall onto a chair and began to cry without restraint.

"Why are you crying? Be happy that your husband is now sitting next to Odin in Valhalla. He has overcome it and will live on as a hero forever".

Helena pulled herself together and jumped up.

"You asshole! See that you get off my farm. You can put your Valhalla wherever you want".

"I'll take this as a typically feminine hysteria attack. See you".

Adolf Wilbers turned on his heel and left the house. Helena stood at the window and watched the notorious Nazi leaving the plot. Then she sat down again and went on sobbing. Only when Antje suddenly stood next to her she got a clear mind again.

"What's the matter, mum? Why are you crying?"

"Well, nothing serious. The bad Uncle Adolf annoyed me. You sometimes cry as well, when the other children annoyed you, don't you"?

Although during the next days, Helena called herself to order several times, she was afflicted by attacks of sobbing now and then. How should she live on without Gerd? How should the farm go on? She has already been completely overcharged, milking cows, feeding horse, removing dung, cooking, washing, ironing, caring for Antje. It didn't only happen once that she was on her feet for eighteen hours without break. Of course her neighbor women helped her now and then. But their husbands were also at the front and each had their own cross to bear.

When the first fall storms blew over the flat country, Helena took the potatoes out of the earth. While Antje enjoying jumped round her, she tore the tufts out of the earth, beat away the dirt, and pulled the potatoes from the leaves. After she had filled her basket, she emptied it onto the bed of her handcart. She worked hard for four full days to bring her potatoes home. Who knew how long and cold the next winter would be? When the first white flakes fell, she had managed it. The hay would be sufficient until the next spring. The turnips were stored. The potatoes were safe in the cellar.

In the beginning of January Adolf Wilbers stood again in front of Helena's door.

"Are the two of you getting well through the winter"?

"What do you want here"?

"Offer you my help. Now and then a man in the house can be an advantage".

"See that you get off here. I don't need your help for sure. I have managed to get along well without you".

"Don't be like that. I brought you some ham. Just bend over and everything will be over"

Helena was entirely confused.

"What shall I do, bend over? Why should I bend over"?

"Well then I lift your skirt, stand behind you and then everything will be fine".

"Why do you want to stand behind me"?

"Tell me are so stupid or do you just pretend"?

"Adolf, either you tell me what you want from me or you disappear at once, got it"?

Adolf didn't tell anything. Instead he did a step forwards, embraced Helena's hips, turned her by one hundred and eighty degrees, roughly pushed onto her back and lifted her skirt. Then Helena did a step forward, stood up again and firmly slapped Adolf's face.

"See that you get out of here at once! Otherwise I will tell the district committee what a nice fellow man they appointed here. Did you understand me, Adolf"?

Adolf stared at Helena with a mixture of astonishment and hostility.

"This you won't dare"

„This I won't dare? I will dare it. If I tell them about your behavior, you will be done. How do you call it so nicely, subversion of the war effort and sabotage? Haven't these been your favorite words for years? And now the discussion is finished. Get lost!"

Adolf struck a blow. His haymaker landed precisely on her left ear. She turned once around herself and stumbled against the kitchen door. Then she sank to the floor.

"What's this going to be? Do you want to kill me"?

"If I had wanted it, you would be dead already. I will tell you something now: as soon as my Manfred will come home, you are going to marry him. Is that clear"?

"Are you entirely insane"?

Helena had picked herself up with an effort.

"Why for heaven's sake should I marry your brainsick son? You show up here uninvited. You try to rape me. You beat the daylights out of my head and on top I should marry your son? Say, have you got a nut loose"?

Again she was hit by a smashing beat. This time her head was hurled against the kitchen door and it got black before her eyes. When she regained consciousness, Adolf lay on her and pumped his seeds into her tummy. She didn't struggle. What could she have done against this sack of potatoes?

When his stink, a mixture of old sweat and cow dung, got into her nose, she turned her head aside and vomited onto the kitchen floor.

"Have you gone completely mad? You can't spit at me like this".

Disgusted Adolf jumped onto his feet, put his penis into his trousers and did a few steps backwards.

"You are going to clean that at once. My son shall take over a tidy farm".

"What do you think your son will say if I tell him what you were doing here just now"?

"You can tell him. I always have a first look at the women he mounts. In this point I have simply more experience".

"You can do what you want, I won't marry your son".

"Yes, you will. I am going to go to the pastor at once and call the banns. As soon as Manfred is back, there will be the wedding. Farm must come to farm. Don't have any illusions about this. This matter is all over for you".

"Get lost! I can't stand having you here anymore".

„Yes, yes, I'm already leaving. But I will come back. You can bet your life on it".

He slammed the door behind him and whistling a song trudged off through the snow.

Helena pulled herself together, cleared her clothes and ran over to her neighbor.

"What did he do to you"?
"He just raped me. And on top I'm supposed to marry his son as soon as he is back".
„He must be crazy. Go to the district committee and talk to them".
Right the next morning Helena set on her way. She had given Anje to her neighbor and thus she made a rapid progress. After only two hours she had reached the district committee in Bremervoerde.
"You want to inform against Adolf Wilbers"?
"He hit me and raped me".
"Young lady, don't talk such nonsense! Wilbers is a good man. He cares for strict discipline. I haven't heard any of this now. Go home and don't give the hysterical lady, ok"?
"But you see how I look like".
"On farms you can easily slip somewhere, especially in winter when it is frozen. Don't tell any fairy tales here. See that you get home and don't steal any of my precious time with your lamentation".
When Helena wanted to reply something, he raised his hand.
"One more made-up story and I will have you arrested. Did I come across clearly enough"?
Helena nodded and left the office with sagging shoulders. This couldn't possibly be true. How should it go on now?

On her way back she collected Antje from her neighbor's.

"You know how I look like, can't you witness for me"?

"I wasn't present, what shall I tell them? And who would like to mess up with the brutal Adolf? I don't want to be put up against the wall. And you know that he is capable of doing things like that".

"Well, I was just an idea".

"I can only give you the advice to keep off the Wilbers. Those people aren't good".

"I would like to do it, but what shall I do when he comes again"?

"Lock your doors. Maybe then he will go again".

Helena took Antje onto her arm and sadly went off. After reaching her farm she locked all doors and shutters. On top she put a knife into each room. Next time she would be better prepared.

Suddenly Helena was rudely awakened. What kind of noise had that been? She carefully listened into the darkness, but wasn't able to hear anything suspicious except Antje's calm breathes. She was trembling all over her body. Did she finally go mad? She decided to calm down at once and sleep on. A busy day was waiting for her after all.

She turned aside, forcefully pushed away her thoughts and got asleep again at last. Suddenly she was torn out of bed and dragged across the room at her hair. She was that much perplexed that she wasn't able to utter any sound. In the neighbor room she was hurled onto the floor. All her bones pained. Suddenly she noticed a smell of alcohol in front of her face.

"Well my little dove, we'll have a round of fun again".

Adolf Wilbers lay on her, pressed her down by his weight, grabbed under his body, spread her legs and repeated what he already had done to her.

"If I were in your place, I would be very peaceful now. You never know what can happen to little children. Your Antje has got such a hole down there as well and you could hide the one or other thing in there, couldn't you"?

That hit. Helena kept laying and hoped that this nightmare would be over soon.

After he had ejected into her, he got up.

"It was good with you. I'll come again for sure. You can already look forward to it."

Then off he was.

Helena pulled herself together, like pulled down by a heavy load she needed several minutes to get onto her feet. She went downstairs, threw a coat over her nightdress and ran to Gertrud, her neighbor. After knocking a few times, the light went on and the door was opened.

"What happened to you? You are trembling all over your body. Come in for now",
Helena entirely frightened slipped by Gertrud into the hall. In the light of the lamp Gertrud was able to see the scale of devastation.
"My goodness, Helena, what did they do to you"?
"Adolf was there again. He raped me and declared he would do the same to Antje if I struggled".
"What a bastard! This is impossible. Where is Antje now"?
"She is sleeping over there".
"Come on, let's go over. We can't let her alone now".
The two women went over to Helena's farm. While Gertrud put on the tea kettle, Helena looked after the little one. Antje was still fast asleep. Helena let her sleep on and went back to the kitchen.
"Helena, it can't go on like this. I will talk to my father in law to talk to Adolf. If I go myself he will only be laughing".
"You would do this for me"?
"Of course".
This night sleeping was impossible. The next day turned out to be according. Helena schlepped through the hours. She didn't think at all. She only functioned. In the evening Gertrud came over.
"My father in law nearly exploded when I told him your story. He went over to Adolf at once and

confronted him. He only laughed at him and advised him to mind his own business in future. Otherwise it could happen that after the next illicit slaughtering some trees could be decorated by hanging men. You see, we tried everything. I don't know any more advice. Maybe you should talk to the old Weber, our pastor".

"Are you sure? I was never able to stand him"

"Just try it. What should happen"?

Right the next morning she went with Antje in tow to the vicarage.

"What did he do to you"?

"He hit me and raped me and threatened to do the same to Antje in case I won't keep quiet".

"Well dear Helena, I'm afraid you are at the wrong address with me. I the bible you can read that the woman has to be subordinate to the man. Your husband has died, so it would be a waste to leave this wonderfully fertile body unused. Don't you think so as well? If Adolf's son Manfred comes back from war imprisonment, as god may make possible, you should quickly marry him. You are only a simple woman after all, to each woman belongs a man. And each woman should give birth to as many children as possible. And now go and apologize to Adolf. He certainly only meant it good with you".

Helena needed a while to find her voice after this speech.

"How did you know about Manfred and me"?

"Adolf called the banns for you already some weeks ago and told me he had decided to engage you and his son together. I didn't have anything against it. After all soil must come to soil and you need a husband who cares about you and makes you many children. So be god-fearing and do what I say. What becomes out of renitent women is well known. They die early or end as a prostitute. And please also think about Antje. What shall become of a small girl without a father"?

With this he cast a wanton glance at Antje.

"Well, little one, you also have a little hole down there, don't you? Wait and see, it will get larger soon and then there will come many babies out of it".

Helena was entirely shocked, took Antje onto her arm, turned round her heel and ran out of the house accompanied by the mocking laughter of the pastor. On her way back she stopped at Gertrud's and told her about the encounter she just had had.

"This isn't true at all, is it"?

"I don't know what to do. I can't just run away. Who should take care of the farm? Where should I go and what should I live on"?

"I have no idea. We can only hope that the war is over soon. Maybe then everything will be better".

From now on Adolf appeared at least twice a week to get his right as he put it. Helena just submitted to the invasiveness. She had tried whatever she could and had failed in every respect. In the course of some weeks something inside her had broken. Her life was over. Only her body still functioned.

"See, my little dove, it isn't all that bad. I brought you two beautiful ones a nice ham. Eat a big piece for now to keep in power. I don't want my son to have to marry a slimmed down mare".

He put the ham onto the kitchen table.

"Well, before I forget it, Antje, from now on you can say granddad to me. Well, be happy. It is good to have a grandfather isn't it"?

Antje stayed silent and only looked frightened at the man.

„Well don't make such a face. I won't bite you. You may come to our farm and play there if you want".

When Adolf was out of the door Helena urgently forbade her daughter to go to Adolf's farm.

"Don't worry mum, this man is bad to you. I won't go there".

*

Someday, Helena and Antje were on their way in the field with horse and wagon, they heard loud motor noises and clank of chain. At once Helena stopped the cart and stood upright onto the platform.

"What is it, mum"?

"The tummies are coming. This damned war is over at last".

Helena took Antje onto her arm and showed into the direction where the noise came from. Two jeeps and a tank came from Bremervoerde along a cart way. Helena sat Antje onto the platform.

"You keep sitting here quietly. Did you understand me"?

Antje hadn't seen her mother that strict and stayed sitting in shock. A few seconds later Helena was on the coach box again, turned the wagon and shood the horse ahead. At high speed they headed for the village. After reaching the farm Helena jumped from the wagon, took Antje down and loosened the reins. While Antje surprised stayed in the yard, Helena shooed the horse into the stable. She left the wagon in the middle of the yard, took Antje under her arm and ran into the house. After having reached the upper floor she put Antje onto a chair.

"Now listen well. The soldiers from England will be here on the farm any moment. I don't know whether they are good or bad. You will stay sitting here and won't move off the spot, ok? I will come and get you as soon as the danger is over".

When Helena looked out of the window she realized that two of her neighbors had already hung white bed sheets out of the upper windows. She left Antje sitting and speeded downstairs. What should she do now? Would the soldiers be friendly to her? What would they do to her? Hopefully they would leave Antje alone. She ran over the yard a bit confused. When she reached the street she realized that Adolf Hilbers had also hung a sheet out of the window.

Well, that was fast, she thought by herself.

After about fifteen minutes the soldiers reached the village. They jumped off their vehicles and searched each house. Helena had run back to the house and waited in the entrance for the appearance of the strange men.

Then it was her house's turn. Without greeting Helena was pushed aside. She heard the noise of many boots in her house. Each room was checked. Suddenly a soldier stood next to her.

"Is that your girl"?

She turned towards the man and realized that he had the entirely frightened Antje on his arm. She immediately reached out and took the girl.

"Is that your girl"?

"I don't understand English".

The soldier went back to his jeep and fetched a book. When he gave it into her hand she realized that it was a dictionary, He took it away again and browsed through it and showed her the word 'daughter'. She nodded.
"Who did this? My soldiers"?
He pointed at the Helena's wounds. Adolf's last visit had only been yesterday. He had hit her again and pulled her through half of the house on her hair.
She thought she understood the question and browsed through the dictionary until she found the word 'mayor'.
"Your mayor did this"?
The soldier looked at Helena in surprise.
Helena nodded.
"Fucking krauts! They are all crazy. But that is not my problem, sorry, madam".
After half an hour the leader called his people together and a few seconds later the troop rushed off the yard.
Many people had secretly longed for the end of the war and had hoped to be conquered by the English or Americans. They certainly wouldn't rage as fiercely the Russians were supposed to do. After all, one was related on a national kind of view, while the Slavs from the east were thought of being capable of everything. There had been enough

records about the cruelties done by these subhuman beings in the far spaces of Russia. Although Nazi Germany had only lasted for twelve years, Hitler's ideology had shaped most of the people. Those who were thinking everything would change right away, were completely wrong, at least for the time being.

Helena had elected the NSDAP as well. She had been taken in by the great fuehrer as well, who had promised everything possible and had held only a fraction of it. Of course, the misery after the World War I had been fatal. Of course the Weimar government had been weak and disunited. Of course she had liked to be taken in by the phrases. But who could have known, what Hitler and his gang had really in mind? Now the German nation had got the acknowledgement. While the great fuehrer had cowardly judged his self while his faithful ones went on the run to South America, the zero hour had chimed for the German people.

Adolf Wilbers had been arrested, but was able to witness his innocence with the help of submissive friends. He was classified as a follower like many others too. To keep the order or reconstruct it, they liked to take back old mayors. Adolf Wilbers, actually a dangerous psychopath, could be extraordinarily obliging, at least towards the new masters. This sudden alignment of his character even lead to the fact, that his son could early leave

English imprisonment. Adolf had talked the Englishmen into believing his farm wouldn't run without his son. As he supplied the occupying forces with food, they pleasantly fulfilled his wish, expressed with tears in his eyes.

Manfred didn't really lack on the father's farm. Adolf several times took advantage of the favorable situation and hoarded enormous amounts of food and animal food. Not all the pigs they had taken from the farmers around had come in useful for the German troops in the East. The one or other had landed in his cellar, cut into pieces or manufactured into sausage of course. Adolf would have been able to live on these supplies for years.

It had come to pass differently and he had simply adapted to the new conditions. He stored the fresh products in his place and sold the stock products to the Englishmen. Thus he cared that the supplied couldn't become too old. Before he had risen to the prince of the province by his brutality, now he could keep his new old status by giving the one or other non-cash benefit.

After the Englishmen had established in the region and built up a small commandant's office, Helena went there again to report about Adolf's intrigues and assaults. However they turned her down there as well.

"You were raped by Adolf Wilbers? Well, then you know now what happened to the Russian women and the women in the concentration camps. Unfortunately I can't do anything for you".

While Helena was so frightened that she almost didn't dare to go to bed in the evening, Adolf talked into his son for hours.

"See that you pinch Helena. I already shot her ready to be stormed. Think of how much land we will get thereto and you will have a wife who will obey".

"No, dad, I don't want her. She is not new. Why should a Wilbers buy a used car when there are so many new ones? Just look at her. She's already worked out and has got the first wrinkles in her face. I'd prefer a beautiful fifteen year old one and I'll teach her working. You can be sure of it".

"What's all this good for? Do you know a fifteen year old girl around here with so much land as Helena has? Don't make a fuss and go over to her. I already called the banns".

After two days Adolf had hiss on convinced more or less. On the third day Manfred went to pay Helena a courtesy visit.

"What do you want here"?

"I want to marry you".

"How did you get to this crazy idea"?

"Because I want to".

"Be honest you don't really want me. Your father wants you to marry me, right"?
"Who wants what is none of your business? I am going to marry you and that's it".
"What if I refuse"?
"Then you'll see what you will get out of it".
"What are you going to do to me"?
The haymaker hit her at her temple. She tried with all her power to keep standing upright, but didn't succeed. She staggered a few steps backwards, crashed into the kitchen door and sank to the floor. After the roaring in her head had ceased a little, she started laughing loudly. Not very long ago she had sat at the same spot on the floor. Should it be her fate to sit on the floor in front of a brutal man?
Before she was able to laugh a second time Manfred was already above her. He tore her on her hair through the hall and upstairs. Then she found herself lying on her bed, her belly exposed. While she was staring into his maliciously smiling face, he undressed his pants.
"Well, have a look. from now on you belong to me. From now on I will do with you what I want. Your husband is dead. He won't be able to help you anymore. So just be reasonable and accept that it is as it is".
While he lay onto her, she turned her head aside. When she felt his brutal stiffness inside her, she

surrendered. She had tried everything, now it was enough. She didn't have any more power to stand against these men. She didn't want to be beaten anymore. From now on she would offer herself voluntarily and hope that it would be over soon. She would try to protect Antje at least.

Adolf Wilbers had been right again in fall the wedding took place. Helena endured it. Helena smiled at her bridegroom and breathed ‚I will'. Helena danced at her wedding. Helena ate and drank and made jokes with the guests. Manfred proudly told everybody who wanted to listen and everybody who didn't want to listen what a great conqueror of women he was. The more alcohol he drank the larger became the property he now presided over.

Only long after midnight the last guests said goodbye. Helena couldn't do anything but steer her freshly married husband into the bed. As he had lashed out when she had been trying to undress him, he finally fell asleep in shirt and trousers. She laid herself in her own bed and quickly fell asleep.

Suddenly she was shaken up.

"What has happened"?

"Don't ask silly questions. My head is going to burst. See that you get me a coffee".

"But I have to cook it first".

"Shut up and hurry"!

Helena immediately jumped out of the bed and ran downstairs to the kitchen. Goodness, why did the water take so long to get boiling? While he shouted for his coffee again and again from upstairs, she poured the hot water carefully through the filter. Don't spill anything now. Don't make any mistakes Quickly she put two cups and the coffee pot onto a tray and took it upstairs.
"I need only one cup. Why did you bring a second one"?
"For me".
"What do you imagine do you really think you will get something of this expensive coffee? I paid it after all".
"This one is of mine".
"Don't talk any nonsense, what belongs to who is clear, isn't it. Since yesterday nothing belongs to you anymore".
She stopped herself from saying anything against it and filled his cup. He took a gulp and burnt his tongue. The cup flew in a high bow across the bedroom and crashed at the wooden wardrobe.
"Do you want to kill me? Look what you caused. How can you give me boiling coffee? And on top one of my best cups is broken now. Come on, see that you get up and clean up this mess. Do you think I want to sleep in a filthy bedroom"?

Without answering she went to get the floor cloth, collected the broken fragments and cleaned the remains of the coffee from the floor.
"Come here"!
Helena stood in front of Manfred's bed.
"Get off your nightdress".
"Well, dewy is something else. But it will be enough for making children. Come on, go to your side and kneel down in front of your bed".
Helena went to her bedside and kneeled down.
"Now let's see what you can offer me".
Manfred got up and kneeled behind Helena. Only after a few strokes she felt his sticky wetness inside her. Without caring about her he got up and ran downstairs. There he was suddenly confronted with the little Antje who sacredly stared at his still dropping semi-stiff genital.
"Get out of my way. I must piss. What are you staring like this? You can't await me making you happy as well, can you"?
He abandoned Antje and ran to the yard to relieve at the dung heap.
In the meantime Helena pulled herself together. What had she heard a moment ago? He wanted to make Antje happy as well? Even though the resistance concerning her own person had broken down but she still wanted to protect Antje. As soon as Manfred had left the house, with Anje in tow she

set her way to Bremervoerde again to make another report at the commandant's office. But also this time she was rejected.

On her way home she went to see her friend to cry on her shoulder.

"See to it that you always keep an eye on Antje." "Send her to us as often as possible or to her playmates next door. When she plays with Guenter, Mathilde and Uwe, nothing can happen to her. I'm sorry that I can't do more for you. Adolf sits firmly in the saddle again and the Tommies won't do anything against him as long as they have him feed them".

*

At Easter 1948 Antje came to school. Because of the turmoil of war everything had retarded a little and so Antje was almost eight years old when she sat at a school desk for the first time. Antje enjoyed school very much. She liked to go there and studied hard. On top Manfred wasn't able to approach her in the morning. Unfortunately Helena wasn't able to always avoid Antje being present when she was hit or raped by Manfred.

"Don't run away, Antje. Look closely then you will know how a real man treats a girl or woman".

Now and then Antje was asked to stand before her mother stooped over and with dress lifted up to enable Manfred a free look on her genital while he raped Helena from behind.

"Yes, keep standing like this. That is good. Wait and see, then you can soon change with your mother".

Antje did what she was told and deadened noticeably. Also in the evenings when Manfred sat in the living room to listen to the radio, she sat on his laps and let him finger her. She didn't care anymore. She endured it and gritted her teeth when he hurt her which sadly happened rather often. She rather had him finger her than have to watch him hitting or raping her mother.

Helena had of course intervened the first times but had given up resistance at a certain point, after he had smashed her to the floor several times. One night she had even taken a knife to the bedroom and firmly intended to put an end to the misery that night. However she had behaved unskillful, the knife had fallen down and Manfred detected it.

"Have you taken leave of your senses"?

Manfred had at once been aware of her intentions and taken the knife. He jumped on her and wrestled her down. Then he put the knife at her throat.

"Be glad that I am a good man. Otherwise I would put your miserable life to an end".

He put the knife on the sideboard, turned her onto the belly and raped her brutally. Afterwards he tore her on her hair onto her feet and pushed her out of the bedroom.

"As a punishment you are going to sleep in front of my door for a few nights"

As she was commanded, she lay onto the hard wooden floor. He had closed the door behind him. She couldn't sleep and was listening the whole night to his loud snoring. Of course she would have been able to get up, open the door and stab him to death. But she wasn't capable of doing it. She had resigned. She didn't want to fight anymore. If there hadn't been Antje she would have killed herself that night.

The months were filled with work. From early in the morning until late at night Helena worked hard on the farm. Of course Manfred helped now and then, but most of the time he spent on the farm of his father.

"My father isn't the youngest anymore and needs help. These few hectares you can easily manage on your own".

"Are you sure that it is only your father who needs help"?

"What do you want to tell me by this"?

"In the village it is told that you are very close to your little sister"
"Who says that"?
"I can't tell you, I heard it here and there".
"Did you? And what is wrong if a brother is close to his little sister"?
"That in your case it doesn't remain with being close".
She landed on the floor again.
"Keep your loose mouth shut otherwise I will forget myself someday. And by the way you can learn a thing or two from my little sister. She's so smashing you can't keep up with her".
In rage he left the house and only returned tanked late at night.

*

At the end of October 1951, Antje had had her eleventh birthday a few months ago, the harvest festival was celebrated. Whereas Helena had to stay at home, Manfred enjoyed himself with a few men of the village in a pub. In the morning they had sat piously in the church and sung holy songs and now beer and corn schnapps flowed freely. Racy jokes made a circuit and caused for roaring laughter all the time.

"Tonight I'm going to break in Antje".

"Have you gone mad? She is only eleven and apart from that this is incest".

"You have got no idea. It can't be incest because she is not my real daughter and with eleven my little sister hadn't been a virgin for long".

"You better take care what you say. If the tommies get to know this, you'll be delivered".

"Duh, stop talking about those bloody tommies. They eat out of the hand of my dad, ha, ha. They won't do me anything".

"What do you say about it, pastor? This isn't right is it"?

"God's paths are sometimes strange. We people are too small to understand all the wonders. Manfred adopted Antje as a father. She is not his real child, but he has to fulfil the duties of a father. How they look like isn't described in the bible".

"Does that mean, pastor, he can do with her whatever he wants? This can't be true, can it"?

"How a father treats his child he has to answer only before god".

"No, no, this is going to be too far for me. I better go now".

"Yes, you fathead, be off to your Elli. We don't need wimps here".

Manfred was completely in his element and felt confirmed by the word of the pastor.

"Think whatever you want. Tonight I'm going to pick the apple. A real man knows where the most beautiful apples are, doesn't he, pastor"?

Only at about two o'clock Manfred stumbled home. However he wasn't capable to fulfil his plan, because always trees, fences and even doors jumped into his way. Tanked he stayed sitting before the entrance door and fell asleep. Only when the morning dawned he came round, picked himself up and stumbled into bed.

*

In spring 1952 Guenter, Antje's play mate became thirteen years old. For the first time he felt more than only friendship for Antje. He often secluded himself from the other children and dwelled on his thoughts. Was it possible that he had fallen in love with Antje? After thinking a lot about it he had to admit this state to himself. This was the cause for seeing Antje with other eyes than before. Instead of playing with her, he often withdrew from her. he was ashamed about his feelings. Didn't boys prefer to play with boys and girls with girls?

"Why don't you play anymore with me, Guenter"?
"Because you are a broad, guys play with guys and broads with broads".
"I don't understand this. We have always got along well with each other".
"Therefore you are too young".
Guenter again and again tried to get Antje out of his mind. However, he succeeded very rarely and if at all only for short times. He went out of her way, but observed her from far. While Antje was playing on the yard of the neighbor, Guenter stood hidden in the bushes and observed the cheerful activities of the girls. Suddenly lout shouting reached his ears.
"Antje, come home at once"
Manfred had appeared at the edge of the yard.
"Come on now or do you need an extra invitation"?
Antje left everything alone and ran towards Manfred. He gave her a spat on the back of her head and pushed her towards his farm. While the other girls went on playing, Guenter sneaked after the two. They disappeared into the house. He sneaked nearer and saw Antje, Helena and Manfred sitting at the table eating supper. Guenter could clearly observe that Manfred who sat at the head of the table hat put his hand on Antje's leg. In the course of only a few minutes he had his hand gliding more and more under Antje's dress. Her dress slipped up little by little. When Manfred had reached his aim,

he smiled at Antje and started to finger in her crotch.

Guenter waited for a reaction of Antje. As there was none, he realized that what he was just observing couldn't be happening for the first time. He ran away in shock. On his way home he thought of how he could help Antje. Then he suddenly knew it. Yes, he would tell it to his mother.

"Don't tell any nonsense, Guenter. You are imagining it. Put a sock in it. You will get us in a hell of a mess".

The next morning he observed Antje on her way to school. She behaved just like the other days. During the lessons he decided to ask the teacher for advice, of course innocuously. After all the children had left the classroom, he stood next to the teacher's desk.

"Well Guenter don't you want to go into your break"?

"Mr. Teacher I have got a question".

"Go ahead, Guenter"!

"I heard that there are fathers who now and then caress their daughters. Is this normal"?

"Yes, that is normal, Guenter. I would call it fatherly love".

"Is this even true if the father caresses her under her skirt"?

"Of course, some fathers caress their children at the shoulders and some do it under the skirt. That's no

problem, Guenter. All fathers do it after all. Aren't you caressed by your parents from time to time"?
"Yes, but rather by my mother".
"Well that's it. You are a boy and you are mostly caressed by your mother. And girls are mostly caressed by their fathers. That is quite common. You don't have to worry about it. And now it's enough. go into the break and play with the other children, I have got still work to do here".
Guenter, didn't believe the teacher, of course his mother caressed him from time to time, but certainly not between the thighs. When he browsed through the women's magazine his mother had subscribed, he came across an agony column. He thoroughly read through the text. The magazine offered the readers to send in a letter with a question or an experience. An expert whose exact subject wasn't described further answered in a letter. Some articles of course anonymized were printed in the magazine.
Yes, that was it. Immediately he sat at the kitchen table and wrote a letter to the magazine. There sat a famous man. He ought to know it. Unfortunately Guenter never got an answer. The magazine didn't pick up the topic either. He felt left alone. Who else could he have asked? A few days later he stayed in the church after the confirmation class.

"Well Guenter, I am happy that you like it in the church".
"Yes, I like it here".
This wasn't true at all but it was an attempt at leniency.
"Well Guenter, be honest. What is your problem"?
"Manfred Wilbers always gropes about under Antje's skirt".
"Under her skirt, you say"?
"Yes, first he caresses her leg and then he pushes his hand more and more under the skirt".
"Did you observe this"?
"Yes, all the three of them sat at the supper table".
"What have you got to do on their farm in the evening"?
"Well I was on my way with friends and then I saw light. And as I was curious I looked through the window".
"And what did you observe there"?
The pastor insistently looked at Guenter. Something had changed. The pastor had been smiling in a friendly way, but this friendliness had completely gone. The eyes of the pastor had become glassy and he seemed to have lost his composure for some seconds.
"What exactly did Manfred do"?
"He put his hands onto Antje's leg and caressed her".

"Did Antje wear stockings"?
"Of course she wore stockings".
"What else did you see"?
"Manfred pushed his hand higher".
"And then the skirt slipped up"?
"Yes, the skirt slipped up".
"So high, that you were able to see the suspenders"?
"Yes, the suspenders were to be seen and then the rest".
"Which rest"?
"Well, you know, just the rest".
"Well, Manfred Wilbers lifted the skirt of Antje so high that you could see the stockings the suspenders and the crotch"?
"Well, exactly, I could see the crotch as well".
"And then"?
"Then he grabbed Antje's crotch".
"And how did Antje react"?
"She didn't react at all. She just went on eating".
"Well, see Guenter then everything is fine".
The pastor had himself under control again.
"What you saw is pure fatherly love, nothing but pure fatherly love".
Guenter didn't feel well near the pastor. Something wasn't right here. with an uneasy smile he rushed out of the church. They could tell what they wanted, fatherly love was different.

Easter approached and Guenter thought of how he could give his adored one a little joy. As he couldn't think of anything appropriate in the early Easter morning he sneaked out of the house, picked some snowdrops and secretly put them onto the sill of Antje's window. We returned home fast in order not to miss the traditional Easter egg hunt. His brothers and sisters found more eggs than him. The reason probably was that he wasn't fully concentrated. What would Antje think if she found the bunch? Did he behave childish or in love? He pondered about it while marching through the garden and searching eggs. Well basically he didn't care about the painted eggs at all. He had other problems after all.

After the Easter mass Manfred enjoyed himself with some other men of the village in the pub. When he returned home for lunch he wasn't fully tanked this time. He had sat next to Antje in the church and secretly caressed her genitals. Today he would pick the fruit and fully drunk this wasn't to be managed so well.

After everybody had taken their seats he spoke the table prayer.

"Come Jesus Christ be our guest and bless what you gave us. Amen".

Helena and Antje replied with the words 'Enjoy your meal'.

Then Manfred took the word.
"Well Lene, what's the matter with you? You always look at me grouchily. Didn't I treat you well? Didn't I love you almost every day? Didn't I fulfill my marital duties well"?
"I think I am pregnant".
"You are pregnant? Did I order you to become pregnant? Why didn't you take care"?
She knew very well, when Manfred talked to her in this voice it was better to keep quiet.
"What is it? Are you pregnant or aren't you"?
„I think I am".
„What does that mean, yes or no"?
"I don't exactly know".
"You don't exactly know? How did you get the idea if you allegedly don't exactly know"?
"Because my menstruation stayed away twice already".
"And you don't tell me"?
"What should I tell you, when I don't know it myself yet"?
Manfred bent forward as fast as lightening and gave her a resounding slap.
"Are you awake now? Well, what is it? Yes, or no"?
"But I don't know it for heaven's sake".
"Will it be a girl or a boy"?
"How should I know"?
Manfred hit her again.

"Stop hitting mum"!
"This is none of your business. Or do you want to be hit as well"?
Antje was silent.
„Come on, speak up! Boy or girl"?
"I am not even sure whether I am pregnant at all. How should I know whether it is going to be a boy or a girl"?
"If it is going to be a boy we will go to Aunt Frida. She will remove the child. I want, if at all, only girls. Ok"?
Helena couldn't do anything but nod. Then they finished their meal in silence. While Helena cleared the table, Manfred caressed Antje's tummy. Suddenly he jumped up and tore Antje with him.
"Don't look that stupid. It is high time that you get to know how lovely it is to be loved by a man".
Antje resisted as much as she was able to, but she had no chance against Manfred. When Helena realized what Manfred was going to do, she threw herself between them. However a hard punch was enough to put Helen out of action. Manfred tore Antje upstairs pushed her onto the conjugal bed and sexually abused her. Although tears ran down Antje's face, she didn't utter a sound. Who knew to what this man had been capable if she had fought?
Suddenly Helena stumbled into the bedroom. After a few more strokes he left Antje, jumped towards

his wife, threw her onto the bed and continued his activities with her. After he had final reached his climax, he rolled aside and fell asleep.
"Mum, it hurt very much".
"Yes, I know Antje. I know that".
"Can't we just go away"?
"Where do you want to go? If they get us, they will bring us back immediately. And you can certainly imagine what he will do to us. Let us be silent about it in future. We don't have any possibility to avoid it. Let it just happen. The less you fight, the less it will hurt and the quicker it will be over".
Although Helena had spoken very intensely to her daughter and Antje had taken her words to her heart, she suffered a lot during the next assaults. She kept quiet. She didn't fight, but the pain which pierced her each time brought tears to her eyes.
After the fifth rape which caused that she wasn't able to sit for two days, she took all her courage and asked her teacher.
"Well little Antje, this is all written in the bible. The woman is subordinate to the man. This is god's will. Don't fight, just enjoy it. I heard that women can have good feelings as well if they don't fight against the iron law of the man".
The teacher put his arm around Antje's shoulders and led her to the restroom. After he had locked the door from inside, he sat onto the bowl.

"Come here, little Antje and show me whether you have become a real woman already".
With these words he tore the entirely confused child onto his knee, pushed her skirt up and started to finger the crotch of the girl. After a few seconds Antje had regained her composure, opened the door and ran off.
"Well, ran little Antje. You can't escape god's will".
"These words bored into her brain. Should the teacher really be right? Was it god's will that girls and women had to submit to the men? When she reached her parent's house, she immediately ran into the living room and took the bible out of the shelf. She browsed and browsed. Then she found the searched spot.
"The woman created out of the rip of the man is subordinate to her husband, has to love and honor him and always fulfil her conjugal duties. Man, birch your wife if she doesn't want to submit. So be it".
After supper Antje went to get the bible.
"Here, dad read this".
Manfred looked at Antje in surprise and read the spot Antje had showed him.
"And what shall I do with it"?
"It is written that the wife has to fulfil her conjugal duties. There's nothing written about a daughter".

"You aren't my real daughter, and if my wife, your mother isn't there, you have to fill in. You are my substitute wife then".
"There is nothing written about a substitute wife".
"It needn't to be written there. If I as a man and landlord say you are my substitute wife then you are my substitute wife, ok? I as a man can do or not do what I want. This is written like that or similarly in the bible. And what is written in the bible is true".
Antje cast a helpless glance to her mother. Helena nodded, she had realized at once that further talking would only have bad consequences.
"Yes, Manfred is right. We have to submit. He is the master in the house. We are only simple women".
For Antje a whole world collapsed. However she didn't have much time to work up her experience. Manfred grabbed round the table and tore Antje onto his lap. He pushed her skirt up and fingered in her genitals. After only a few moments he pushed Antje down, opened his trousers to set Antje onto his stiffness a few seconds later. Antje didn't fight she even whipped up and down a few times to satisfy his desire as fast as possible. After he had emptied himself inside her he pushed her aside.
"See, we are going to do it like that always. It is quite easy, isn't it"?

From now on Antje didn't fight anymore. As soon as Manfred approached her, she bent down to offer herself to him.

"Not now. Don't you see I have to work? You can't wait for being loved by me again, can you"?

Antje didn't do it to endear herself or because she enjoyed it. She did it to discharge her mother. When made her available, Manfred left her mother alone.

*

"Tell me, Helena, where are actually the cadastral plans of this farm"?
"What do you want with them"?
"That is none of your business, thus, where are the plans"?
"They are in the desk standing in the attic".
"Go and get them for me".
Helena obeyed immediately to avoid the hits she would get otherwise and fetched the plans. Without answering Helena's asking looks he put the plans into a brief case and left the house. After about two hours he returned.
"You must sign here".
"What do I have to sign"?
"The contract, or does it seem to be a milk bill"?

"What kind of contract is this"?
"I'm going to sell a bit of farmland to the church. They had been keen on it for long".
"You can't just sell a slice of farmland to the church. First of all it is my land and secondly Antje should inherit all of it once".
"Since when have you been asked for your opinion? Sign and do hurry up".
"No, I certainly won't sign this. I won't watch you selling half of the farm. By the way what do you want to do with the money"?
"Modernize, what else"?
"What do you want to modernize here"?
"This is none of your business. Sign before I forget myself".
Helena shook her head. This gesture caused Manfred to jump round the table and threw Helena from the table with a massive haymaker. He bent over her and tore her up at her hair and dragged her upstairs into the bedroom. After the usual rape he tore Helena back to the kitchen.
"Sign now or I will kill Antje".
"You want to kill Antje. Then you will go to jail".
Again Helena was thrown off the chair again.
"You will both have an accident. Things like that happen on farms. Sometimes a stave breaks or somebody falls into the hay and suffocates. Such a farm is a dangerous place of work.

"You won't dare it"
"You can bet your life on it. Actually a good idea. Poison kills safely and soundless. Maybe you have nibbled rat poison, of course quite unintentionally. Things like that are said to have already happened, haven't they"?
Helena wiped the blood from her nose and her chin and signed. And it shouldn't be the last signature. After Manfred had sold another field and two meadows, he finally bartered away the horse to buy a tracker.
On top of this he allowed himself a private cure every few months. In a famous health resort he met his father and his little sister. For himself be brought Antje. For two weeks Antje and Manfred's sister were living with their fathers in two hotel rooms next to each other and the men proudly showed up with the young ladies in public.
Now and then the girls were sent away. The men undisturbedly wanted to talk about business.
„Tell me Manfred, what do you make of it if I introduce you to my major? He signalized me that he is looking for a further supplier. If that works, you will be set for life. You feed some more pigs and business will be going well".
Manfred agreed at once and bought a few more pigs from the neighbor farms to sell them to the

Englishmen with a good and proper price premium. With the money he refurnished the house.
"Why do you spend so much money on furniture? The old ones are still sufficient".
"Helena, since when you have been asked for your opinion? Just shut up and everything will be fine, ok"?
Manfred wasn't to be deterred and bought a new kitchen, a new living room, a new dining room and a new bedroom. Further he had all the walls redecorated and the doors and window frames newly painted. Helena wondered. What could this mean?
A few days later she realized why Manfred had been so keen on the new furnishings. When she came out of the stable shortly before supper, a few men were standing on the yard.
"What do you all want here? Is there anything for free"?
"Your Manfred invited us. He is going to be forty today, didn't you know"?
Helena recalculated in her head. Dear goodness, the men were right. It was Manfred's fortieth birthday today.
Suddenly Manfred came out of the door.
"Come in, we want to celebrate today".
He tuned on his heels and stopped in the door to have all men pass him.

"Say Manfred why didn't you tell me that we are expecting guests. I haven't prepared anything".
"You misunderstood something. They are not our guests but mine, ok? And you don't need worry about the celebration. I cared for everything. And before I forget it, I don't want to see you down here tonight. This is my celebration and I won't have it destroyed by you. You can sit in the stable if you want and wait until we will be finished. Or you can go to bed right now. I don't care, but if I consider it well, I think it is better you will stay in the stable. You needn't know everything we will talk about".
"And where will Antje stay"?
"She will stay with me. She can help the waitress".
"Which waitress"?
"The one to come in a moment".
"You engaged a waitress"?
"The Tommies sometimes have delivered food from the Hotel Behrends. I asked there, they also deliver to one's home now and then. They will come any moment and deliver the food".
"Have you gone completely crazy? Who shall pay for this"?
"Well me, who else"?
"But you can't so this".
"Discussion is over. You know where your place is. And don't dare to disturb us, ok? Or do you want to end in the cesspool? It is said to be quick if you fall

into it. The gases aren't very healthy I was told. Well go to the stable and sit on a stool. I will tell you as soon as we will be finished".

In order to avoid a further beating attack Helena surrendered at once. Shortly before eight o'clock a complete dinner was delivered indeed. She sat on her stool and observed the activities in front of the house and then inside. Manfred had pushed two tables together and fetched a third one from the kitchen. The waitress and Antje ran around the tables and filled the glasses and the plates. At a late hour, the gentlemen were already beyond good and evil, they sang energetically and loudly. While the men roared in choir, Manfred gave the beat with a cooking spoon.

Suddenly she saw the waitress on the table. The young woman danced and all the men clapped the beat. Now and then one of the men lifted her skirt and Helena was able to see the exposed genitals of the woman, framed in suspenders and stockings.

Suddenly Manfred shouted "Antje, Antje, Antje".

Now Antje had to dance on the table as well. Manfred was really enthusiastic and shouted again and again "Well, don't I have a gold child with me? You are all envious, aren't you"?

A few gentlemen seemed to be irritated.

"Well, don't look so embarrassed. She has been broken in for long. Come on Antje, show us what you can offer".

Manfred stepped to the table and lifted Antje's skirt. Antje knew what would happen if she didn't obey now, went on dancing.

Suddenly Manfred shouted "undress, undress, undress" and a few men joined in. While the waitress performed a skillful strip and finally danced only in bra, girdle, stockings and pumps, Antje stood next to her like rooted to the spot. Before she could react at all, Manfred had lifted her from the table and undressed her skirt. Then he lifted her back on the table.

"Don't make such a fuss and start dancing. We want to see something".

Antje, now with exposed genitals herself, copied the waitress and danced on the table to the singing of the men.

"We want to see tits, we want to see tits"!

The waitress didn't put herself on hold and removed her bra. This gesture was honored by loud applause.

"Antje, Antje, Antje"!

Then Manfred stepped in.

"It is pointless. She is still as flat as a board".

After about half an hour both of them went down the table. The men were so tanked by now that they

didn't realize that the waitress and Antje had got dressed again and removed the dishes.
Helena had observed everything from outside and hadn't stepped in. What could she have done?

*

Several times Guenter put flowers onto Antje's window spill, but didn't have the courage to talk to her. This couldn't go on like that. One evening when Antje stood together with her friends he took all his courage and approached the group.
"Antje, I have to talk to you. Can you come with me to the back of the house"?
Antje had known Guenter for many years and followed him.
"What's the matter Guenter? What do you want"?
"I like you very much".
"Is this what you wanted to tell me"?
"Yes, that's what I wanted to tell you".
"I like you too".
"Do you want to be my girlfriend"?
"I would like to but if my stepfather gets to know it, he will kill me".
"Well we'll manage this. We don't have to tell anybody. By the way, did you like the flowers"?

"I've already thought that you were behind it. I observed you several times observing me".
"You noticed it"?
"Well to be able to sneak like a Red Indian you will still have to exercise a bit more".
"Agree"?
"Agree to what"?
"Well are you my new girlfriend or aren't you"?
"Well ok, but it must be a secret".
"So you are my new girlfriend now and we have a secret"?
„Yes, you could say so".
Guenter brushed Antje's forehead with his lips, blushed and ran away. After a few moments Antje had calmed down as well and returned to her friends.
"What did this bloody Guenter want from you"?
"Well he told me that he doesn't understand German. The lyrics of Schiller are not in his line".
From now on Antje and Guenter secretly met several times a week behind an old shed. Sometimes they talked to each other for a while. Sometimes they only stood together in silence and enjoyed their togetherness. Antje had detected a loose stone in the shed's wall. When you pulled it out, there was a little hole. This tiny hollow they both started to use for secret messages. Many a hot love letter waited there for its reader.

Shortly before Antje's fourteenth birthday Helena gave birth to a son. Manfred ran riot and beat onto his wife in rage.

"How can you dare to give birth to a son? Didn't I tell you often enough that I want only daughters"?

If the midwife had not energetically gone between them Manfred would have beaten his wife to death.

"Have you gone completely mad? Your wife just gave birth to a child and you are beating onto her as if she would be a lazy dobbin. What a brute you are"!

"Shut your cheeky mouth, midwife. This is none of your business I treat my wife like I want and like she deserves it".

"You are off your rocker. Even you should know that neither man nor woman can influence the gender of a child. Didn't your mother tell you? Don't blow up like this otherwise I will forget myself".

Manfred raised his hand to stop in the last moment.

"Dare it once, you coward. Beating women is what you are able to? What do you think will happen if I send you my Wilhelm? He will eat you for breakfast, my dear".

Manfred cleared his way. He rather didn't want to mess up with Wilhelm, the gigantic husband of the midwife.

"Look at him, Helena. Now he chickens out, this coward".
"You better shut your mouth now. What do you think he will do with us after you have gone"?
"How you bear with this fathead. Not even ten horses would be able to keep me here".
"Where should I go? When I leave nothing will belong to me anymore. Should I walk the streets in Hamburg to bring through me and my children"?

*

1954 Guenter finished school. His father had found him an apprenticeship in a neighbor village fifteen kilometers away. He would have liked to become a farmer, but as the second born son he didn't have a chance to inherit the parental farm. As his way to work was too long for a daily foot march, he had to stay with his boss during the week. Now and then when his fully filled workday allowed it, he borrowed a bicycle to be able to visit Antje. Several times he waited in vain behind the shed. Sometimes for weeks they only exchanged love letters they placed behind the loose stone.
Shortly after her fifteenth birthday Antje had her first visit of Aunt Irma and Manfred shouted about

his bloody trousers after the evening assault. From now on he left the girl alone.

A few days later Antje and Guenter met and were standing behind the shed embracing each other tightly. Suddenly a stone flew by Antje's head only a few centimeters and smashed into the shed's wall. Both were scared to death. Even before they realized what had happened, they saw Manfred running towards them. Manfred with his face red of rage pushed Guenter down to the earth and slapped Antje's face. Then he turned round as lightening, linked arms with Antje and tore her off with him. Guenter was shocked and needed some time to stand up again. He ran after the two and caught them up. When Manfred heard him come, he turned round to him.

"Should I catch you two once again, you will have had it. And now Guenter see that you get home and leave my Antje alone".

Manfred turned again and tore Antje behind him. When they reached their yard he left her and beat her like mad. If Helena hadn't gone between them in the last moment, he would have beaten Antje to death.

After Helena had received a few strong punches, he tore both women into the house.

Guenter, who had followed them, had to watch helplessly what Manfred did to the women.

Guenter who certainly wasn't a coward realized at once that intervening of his side would have deteriorated everything.

However Antje and Guenter weren't able to leave each other. They met as often as possible, sometimes at the edge of the wood, sometimes hidden behind the shed. The gentle affection of the beginning had become real love. Manfred could rage and thrash about Antje had lost her heart to Guenter.

To finish this love affair Manfred had contacted a farmer in Lueneburg with the help of his father. Adolf Wilbers and Kurt Leupert had met on a meeting of the British Army. Both of them delivered food to the Englishmen.

Kurt and Manfred soon came to an agreement. A few days later Antje had to tie up her bundle. Manfred and Antje got into a train in Bremervoerde and a few hours later they reached the farm of Mr. Leupert.

"Make her work properly and wipe this nonsense out of her brain. She mustn't mess about with boys, she must learn to work".

"Don't worry, Manfred. We will manage it. Antje is not my first apprentice. We saved other situations as well believe me".

While Antje unpacked her things in her small room under the roof, Manfred said good bye and went back to Bartelshain. Manfred had been hardly out of sight when the farmer suddenly stood in her small room.

"You heard what your father said. Come on, you are not on vacation here".

"I'm a little exhausted by the train ride. And by the way Manfred isn't my father. My father didn't come back from war".

"This is none of my business. For me Manfred is your father and now see that you get into the stable. Exhausted by the journey? Don't make me laugh. You were idly sitting in the train all the time. What would you young thing be exhausted from"?

Kurt grabbed and rudely tore Antje towards him.

"If you are a little friendly to me, it will be easier for you. If not, you' will see what will be your reward".

As Antje tried to free herself from his hug, he harshly turned her and pushed her out of the room. He hardly had fallen downstairs but was able to grab the handle in the last moment.

When Antje came downstairs staggering, she had almost crashed into the farmer's wife.

"Say Kurt, are you crazy? Leave your fingers from the girl or do you want to be given the gate of this farm"?

"Why should I be given the gate of this farm"?

"Maybe, because this is my farm"?

"Darling, I don't know what's wrong with you. I only wanted to be friendly to our new housemate".
"Leave the girl alone, ok? Otherwise I will forget myself someday. And you certainly don't want to experience this, do you"?
Lisa linked arms with Antje and just left her husband.
„Don't worry he won't do you any harm. Should he approach you in spite of my warning, tell me. Then I will hang him onto the next tree. I can't think what came over me when I married him. Well, now it is too late anyway, we both have to live with it".
Antje was very much released about this twist and gave her best to please the farmer woman. But as much as she tried to suppress her desire for Guenter, she had to think of him again and again.
"What are you dreaming about here? See that the cows are milked. Don't think that you are here on vacation only because my wife likes you".
Someday Antje was troubled by an enormous shower of longing. She stabbed the pitchfork into the dung heap and ran behind the barn to set her tears free unobserved by anybody.
Suddenly Kurt stood behind her, grabbed her from behind and embraced her breasts. Antje kept standing as stiff as a statue. She was so much startled that she wasn't able to fight back or even utter a sound. Kurt pushed harder. The pain

brought Antje out of her scared stiffness and she cried out loud.

"Shut your mouth. Do you want to hound the others towards us"?

Suddenly there was a shouting from behind.

"Kurt, keep your hands off the girl. Are you deaf or what? Take your hands off".

Antje heard the farmer woman approach. Then suddenly the farmer's hands disappeared off her bosom. Instead Kurt shouting glided down her. Antje turned round in shock. Kurt lay on the ground crying. His wife stood above him threateningly.

"Have you gone completely mad? You could have killed me".

Lisa Leupert stood above him unaffected and supported on her hay fork.

„You can be sure that next time you won't only get a hit on your shoulder. Next time, if there should be one at all, I will lance you and hang you onto the next tree on your scrotum. So everybody will be able to see with what swine I have to live here".

"You won't dare it".

"You can bet your life on it that I will dare it. This was the last warning. I hope you did understand me".

Kurt jumped onto his feet and threateningly stood before his wife.

"What do you want, you clown, huh, threaten me or what shall this become? See that you get to your work, you piece of dirt, before I forget myself".

To show Antje who was the master in the house Kurt raised his hand. His fist didn't land in Lisa's face however, but on the stick of the fork. Lisa had lifted the fork as fast as lightening and stretched against him. Howling of pain Kurt stood before his wife.

"Haven't you still got enough? What should this become? Do you want to beat your wife? You are a real hero. The Russians should have killed you. Then I would have got rid of you. See that you scram. As I said before next time it's your turn".

Lisa stepped a pace back and held her fork against him. Then she did a very quick step towards him. He side stepped her mock assault in shock and ran off.

"Well, we are rid of him for now. He will sleep in the broom closet in future. Or do you think I let him in my bedroom? Who knows what thoughts he will get.

Now tell me, what is the matter with you? Are you pregnant or what"?

Antje couldn't but approach Lisa, hug her and uncontrollably cry. After she had calmed down a little she told the farmer woman the whole story of her life.

"Well you are in love with Guenter then and Manfred sent you here to separate the two of you? Well, we will play a good trick on him. I don't get rid of the feeling that men are all crazy. It is only about property. We women aren't worth more than a horse or a cow, we shall obey all the time and be on service and for heaven's sake have no own opinion, haven't we? Well, am I silly or what? It can't go on like that with you. See that you write your Guenter a letter. He certainly is as bad patched as you are, isn't he"?

Although Antje at once wrote a letter to her loved one, the letter reached his new address only after two weeks.

"Guenter come quickly down the ladder".

Guenter heard his boss shouting from down and stepped down the rungs.

"What's the matter, boss?"

„Here's a letter from an Antje from Lueneburg. Where from do you know women from Lueneburg"?

Without answering Guenter tore the letter out of his boss's hand and happily ran out of the house of a customer. Behind the house corner he sat onto a pale of wood and several times turned the letter in his hands. Then he finally dared to open the envelope. Antje reported about her experiences and

finished the letter with the words 'I love you and I incredibly long for you'.
Tears of joy filled his eyes and he decided to visit her.
"Guenter, Guenter, where are you? The conduction must be finished".
Only after the third call Guenter emerged out of his thoughts and ran back to his boss.
"Boss, I have to have some days off, by all means".
"What is the matter? Are you becoming a father or what? Aren't you a bit too young for this"?
"No, boss, I don't become a father. I want to visit my Antje in Lueneburg. Please, boss, give me a few days off".
"And what does your father say to it"?
"No idea, I'm going to ask him".
"If your father agrees, you can go as far as I am concerned".
Guenter was beside himself with joy and just wanted to run off, when his boss called him off.
"First we will finish this task, ok? You can't just leave everything behind. But do it reasonably, if you please".
"Yes, boss"
While Guenter quickly climbed the ladder, his boss stayed down and smiled to himself. He had been young himself after all and now and then loved to remember his love affair with his current wife.

However it should take several weeks until Guenter was able to realize his idea. As his small wages of an apprentice weren't enough for a train journey to Lueneburg, he had frenetically searched for another solution to get to Lueneburg. Finally he found one. One of his school mates had just become eighteen and had made his driver's license. On top Jochen worked as a car mechanic and thus had access to the one or other company vehicle. As Guenter's parents didn't have any objections, on a Sunday morning the two young men set for the way to Lueneburg.

When after many hours they finally arrived at the farm of the Leuperts, they only met Kurt coming out of the stable.

"Who do you want to, to Antje? There's no Antje living here".

„What nonsense are you talking? Come on in".

Lisa waved from the kitchen door to the two travelers.

Guenter and Jochen looked at each other astonished and just left Kurt to follow Lisa's invitation.

"Sit down here in the kitchen, I will go and get Antje".

While Guenter and Jochen took a seat, Lisa rushed towards the stable. Antje was just throwing the dung onto a cart.

"Come to the house as soon as you are ready. I think a very pleasant surprise is waiting for you".
Lisa left the shocked Antje and ran out of the stable. As soon as she had shut the door behind her, she broke out into an almost whinnying laughter. She pulled herself together. Hopefully Antje hadn't heard anything.
Lost in thought Antje went on shoveling. What bad could have happened? When she approached the dung heap with the full cart, she saw a strange car. How did that car come here? Should she be taken off? But why should she? She didn't do anything wrong after all. After she had tipped the dung, she rounded the strange car. According to the plate the car had to come from Bremervoerde. Bremervoerde? Manfred had come to collect her. Not he police had come to tell her that Manfred had killed her mother. No, this couldn't be true. Didn't policemen drive about in green cars? Maybe policemen used a civil car for longer tours. Antje was about to die when she finally arrived in the kitchen. There sat two men and talked to Lisa.
"Well there you are at last. Dear goodness what's the matter? Did you linger"?
Lisa glanced smilingly towards her.
„Look who has come".
Antje was completely taken aback. Then she finally realized who was sitting in the kitchen. Guenter

jumped up and ran towards her. Both of them met with impact and held each other as if there would be no tomorrow.

"See that you get out of the door. You certainly have to tell each other a lot".

Guenter and Antje stood in the middle of the kitchen with tears in their eyes.

"See that you get out of here".

Antje was the first one to compose herself, linked arms with Guenter and tore him out of the kitchen, through the hall, through the backdoor into the garden.

"Well, we won't see the two of them for a long while, don't you agree, Jochen"?

Antje told Guenter what she had experiences on the Leupert's farm. She didn't even leave out Kurt's approaches and Lisa's reaction to them. Both several times burst out in laughter about Kurt's silly face. What Manfred had done to her she didn't tell anything. Antje had decides a long time ago not to mention these sexual assaults, as she feared Guenter would leave her. Already years ago he had heard that men would prefer women who go into marriage as a virgin.

Only late in the evening Guenter and Jochen drove home after a farewell full of tears. Guenter as well as Antje were very sad about this new separation, but lived on this joyful meeting for weeks.

*

They had however made their calculation without Kurt. Kurt, still in rage, hadn't been able to do any better than writing a letter to Manfred, telling him about the visit of Guenter. However he didn't only report the facts, but invented the one or other incident. Among others he told Manfred that Guenter and Antje had spent about two hours alone in the hay.
Manfred was off the wall after he had read Kurt's letter.
"Your daughter is a whore. She will suffer for this. How can she just jump into the hay with this nonentity? This will have consequences".
Like always when he was in rage Helena had to suffer. Like being out of his senses he beat onto the defenseless woman just to rape her again after a few minutes.

*

To distract himself from the desire for Antje Guenter began to play accordion. He exercised as often his rare free time mad it possible and detected completely new sides within himself. He was talented and just played some things off his soul. Now and then he performed on little celebrations and thus earned a few marks extra.

A few weeks later he had enough money to pay Antje another visit. The joy of seeing each other again was great of course.

"This can't go on like that".

"What do you want to change? My time on this farm hasn't been over for long. I won't be able to come and see you. Firstly I don't necessarily want to stay in Manfred's house and secondly I won't get free for a whole week and thirdly I don't have money to pay for the train".

"What about marrying"?

"You want to marry me"?

"Well of course I want to marry you".

"You better think twice. I am not really rich and not at all beautiful. How do you imagine this"?

„You are the most beautiful and most intelligent girl in the world. And you needn't be rich. I don't earn very much, but as soon as I will be fully trained it will be enough for the two of us".

Almost every weekend Guenter played dance music and every few weeks he afforded a rail journey to Lueneburg. Now and then he was also able to get Jochen being interested in a trip. But in February 1958 Jochen put him off.

„With this weather you will have to take the train. I don't want to sit in any ditch with the car of my boss".

Guenter bought a ticket and set on his journey. In the meantime he had finished his apprenticeship and this time he wanted to do the job properly. Right this afternoon he would ask for Antje's hand. Of course he was aware that there would be problems. Manfred wasn't well-disposed for him at all. But somehow he would manage it. He puzzled it over and over. What words did a young man use to talk a young woman into saying yes?

"Hi Antje, do you want to marry me"?

No, this seemed to be too casual.

"Antje, I love you and I want to marry you, What do you think about it"?

Not really well either.

"My dearest Antje would you consider to marry me"?

Maybe this was a bit too stilted wasn't it? Oh dear, it couldn't be too difficult. Then he found it, yes, he wanted to do it just like that.

Finally after hours they stood in front of each other.

"Antje, please come with me behind the barn".

"What is it so secretly"?

"Antje, I love you and I want to marry you, preferably now and on the spot. Do you want to marry me as well"?

"Is this supposed to be an official proposal"?
Guenter actually didn't easily get himself worked up but felt how he blushed. He clenched his teeth.
"Yes, you won't believe it but other people call it wedding proposal".
"Are you really serious about it"?
"As serious as I have never been in my life. Well what is it, yes or no"?
"Dear goodness, are you in a hurry".
"Yes, I am. I want to have you finally and forever with me. I want to love you and honor you until death do us apart. And by the way, I don't want to travel here and there all the time".
"I see, that's your point. The voyages are too expensive for you".
"What are you talking about? Each weekend I stand in some pub and play my heart out, so that I can visit you".
"Calm down again. It was only a joke".
"Well what is it then"?
"My dear Guenter, nothing would be further for me than to say no now".
Guenter was irritated.
„What does that mean? Can't you speak proper German to me? You know that I am a simple craftsman".
"Yes"!
"Yes"?

"Yes"!

"Dear goodness, couldn't you have said it immediately? I am stammering about here and you are joking about me".

"Well my dear this is a great start, not even properly married and already the first marital quarrel".

"Marital quarel"?

"Man, what's the matter with you? You have never been so humorless".

"I think I was a bit over challenged. During the whole journey I thought about how I could ask you. And then I finally got it and you are joking about it and let me dangle".

"Have you understood now? I love you and I declare loud and clear yes. Is this cleared up now"?

"Then we are engaged now"?

"It is commonly called so".

"How snippy you are? I don't do you anything bad".

"Well it's the excitement. You won't believe it but I don't get a wedding proposal every day".

"You don't"?

"I don't".

"I am surprised".

"Why"?

"Because I have been convinced, that girls of your quality are awash with wedding proposals every day".
"You are an idiot".
"Honestly, how are we going on"?
"You are asking me? I thought you were thinking the whole journey about it".
„I thought about the wedding proposal, I wanted to discuss the rest with you".
"Well that's what it is. First acting the grandiose gentleman and then not knowing how to go on. You are a real hero. What do you suggest"?
„I will call the banns in Bartelshain".
"Don't we both have to present at calling the banns"?
"No idea, I will clear this".
"Then do it and then we will see further".

*

Guenter, who had changed his job in the meantime to earn more money, was taken aside by his boss on the Monday after his last journey to Lueneburg.
"Guenter, we must move with the times. I don't want to go to the customers with a motorbike and a

trailer. I decided to buy two small motor trucks. Do you actually have a driver's license"?
"No, boss, I haven't had the money for it yet".
"I could pay for it how does that grab you? Then we both could drive to the customers with the motor trucks. We would be quicker, would reach the customers easier, could take more tools and spare parts and on top of it make more money. It won't be to your disadvantage".
"Count me in, boss. When will it start"?
"I have already registered you. You can start next week".
Guenter was of course very much pleased. Maybe he even could lend the truck for a weekend to visit Antje. He put his shoulder to the wheel and learned all the traffic rules in a minimum of time. He didn't mind driving itself and thus he passed his exam after a short time.
"Well done, Guenter, congratulations to the new driver's license. Just turn a few rounds on the yard. Tomorrow morning you will do your fist customer's visits with it".
Guenter got in. He was a bit afraid. The truck drove differently than the tiny car in which he had absolved his driving lessons. Dear goodness this thing was heavy to steer. That was going to be hard work.

When he reached his first customer the next morning and repaired a power supply line he had an idea. The village he was just in had a register office. Shouldn't he ask right away what documents he needed to get married? In addition asking here would prevent his matter to be known in his home village. Manfred had to be informed in advance by all means.

At ten o'clock he had his breakfast break. But this time he didn't just stay in the driver's cab to eat his bread, but drove to the town hall right away to get informed. There he learned that a ban had to be called by each of the ones wanting to get married. They also told him which documents were necessary and they had to prove the full legal age.

The documents shouldn't be a problem. But how would he be able to take Antje to the register office without Manfred knowing about it? in the evening he called the Leuperts. His boss had had an own telephone for a few months and had allowed Guenter to use it now and then. The Leupert's family had had a telephone for two weeks as well. This made it much easier for Guenter and Antje to communicate.

Lisa was on the phone and immediately got Antje out of the stable.

"Hello, my dear. Isn't it great such a telephone, is it"?

"The best invention since the printing of books or so".
"Is there anything new with you"?
"I was in Langen at the register office and asked about our wedding banns. We have to bring a few documents. This will be no problem".
"What's the problem"?
Guenter heard Antje's fearful voice.
"I can't all the banns on my own. You have to be present as well. Furthermore we will need the allowance of our parents, as we both aren't twenty one yet".
They talked to each other for more than an hour. Then they had concocted a bold plan

*

A few days later Guenter drove to Lueneburg in the car of his friend and collected Antje. Lisa had told Kurt that Antje wanted to visit her parents. Guenter drove directly to Jochen. Jochen had been brought to the loop of course and provided his room for the two of them. This night the two of them got very near to each other. Right the next morning Guenter took Antje to the station in Zeven. There she got into the train to Bremervoerde and there was collected by Manfred.

"It's about high time that I have you home again. Your mother is that worn that I don't have fun anymore".

"You can forget about it. These times have gone forever".

"What does that mean"?

"I am not available anymore. I talked to Lisa Leupert about you and she told me she will accuse you at once, if you grab me once more".

"To whom does she want to accuse me? Doesn't Kurt have a handle on this silly cow"?

"Lisa clearly told him that he is living on her farm and that she will give him the chop if he doesn't toe the line".

"What has happened to him? I don't know him like this at all".

"Lisa said she will tell the Englishmen what kind of you are, if you don't leave me alone. She will care that you will be crossed of the list of suppliers of the Englishmen. And furthermore she will care that you will at once be sent to jail in case you approach me. I can only warn you".

Manfred had lost his composure for a short time. However she wasn't able to judge whether he was angry because of her talk or afraid because of the threatening. Having arrived at the farm she firstly hugged her mother. Helena had got visibly older. The permanent mockeries, the daily beats, the rapes and the birth of two further children had left their imprints. She was in the beginning of her forties now and could have easily been judged for sixty.

When they sat together for a meal Antje took the word.

"And what I also wanted to tell you, I will marry Guenter".

"What will you do"?

Manfred was beside himself.

"I will marry Guenter".

"No way. As long as your feet are under my table you will do what I say. The wedding won't take place and period".

"Dear Manfred, I think you mixed up something".

"Uh-huh what is it"?

"You are putting your feet under my table".

"Enough is enough. Have you gone completely mad? What nonsense are you telling here"?

"I informed myself. Nothing here belongs to you and neither to your children. And if you wouldn't be married to my mother, I would send you off the house".

Manfred boiled over and jumped up to slap Antje.

"Well Manfred, go ahead. You know what will happen then. Well, you super courageous guy, go ahead, beat defenseless women. You can give the

hero with us. I heard you aren't that hyped-up towards men".
Manfred sat down again in rage.
"Well, from the beginning again, I will marry Guenter and that is it".
"We'll see that. You aren't fully aged and until you will be fully aged there will be no marriage".
"This is not true. If Mum agrees it's all over".
"Your mother won't agree".
"Yes, she will".
„I will know how to avoid this. The final chapter has not been written yet".
Right the next day Manfred set for his way to Bremervoerde to call on the district court. There he knew an employee who owed him a favor.
"This is very easy. You declare your wife for being mentally incompetent and then I have to appoint a custodian for Antje. In the worst case I could so it myself. Then we could be sure that everything runs as we want it".
With his head held high and utterly satisfied with himself he returned to the farm.
"You will get a custodian now as your father is dead".
"My mother will be enough".
"No she isn't. I talked to the district court. You will get a custodian and he will care that you can forget about your marriage with Guenter".

At midnight Antje and Guenter met behind the barn. After the first bear hug Antje told what Manfred had done to avoid the wedding.

"He is a really bloody bastard. I will talk to my parents. Maybe something can be done".

Right the next morning Guenter informed his parents.

"You want to marry Antje? Well this is great. She is just the right one for you. And we will give Manfred a piece of his mind".

The very morning Guenter and his father set for their way to the district court.

„My son Guenter wants to marry Antje. Is anything said against it"?

"Nothing actually, however she isn't twenty one yet and the custodian has decided that a wedding is out of question".

"Who is the custodian"?

"I took this task myself, As a custodian you have a great responsibility for your ward, so I preferred to do it myself".

"Uh-huh, and you refuse it? Why actually? My son has got a steady job he earns enough to feed a family. And on top we are there as well".

"This is exactly the point. Is Guenter really able to supply a family on his own? He is not very old after all".

"He is able to do it".

"I am not so sure about it. Women are demanding, we both know this for sure. Now imagine Antje wants a new bedroom or a new kitchen. Would Guenter be able to afford this"?

Guenter's father looked at the officer irritated.

"Se, you have got your doubts as well, haven't you"?

"No, I don't have doubts. You are just talking nonsense".

"You can see it as you like. I say no and I won't change my mind. Sometimes you have to protect the young people before themselves. They marry quickly, then the first child comes and then they are a bit short of domestic bliss because the mother wants to have new diapers or anything else. No, no and no again".

"Who is your boss"?

"I don't have to tell you. I am in charge here and nobody else".

"We'll see".

On their way back they stopped off at an inn.

"Could I use your telephone please"?

"Sure it is there at the end of the counter".

"Do you also have a telephone book for me"?

"Sure it is on the small table text to it".

While Guenter ordered two beers at the counter, his father browsed through the telephone book. Then

he found what he had looked for and dialed a number".
"Attorney's office Schulz and Muller, hello, what can I do for you"?
"It is about a marriage of minors. The stepfather is against it and asked a custodian for help. How could we bypass his objection"?
"By contacting his boss".
"Where can I find him"?
"He is in the court. It's the family judge".
"Thank you very much for your information. You helped me a lot".
Guenter's father put down the receiver just to browse in the telephone book again and dial a number.
"District court Bremervoerde, hello".
"I would like to talk to Judge Jansen".
"In what matter"?
„It is about an adoption".
"I think he has already gone. Wait a moment. I'm going to check if I can get him".
After several cracks the judge was on the line.
"Jansen".
Guenter's father explained the situation to the judge and asked for a talk.
"Come on Monday to the court, then I will have time for you".

After both had drunken and paid for their beer, they went home. Right the next morning Guenter would ask his boss for a day off.

Hardly at home Guenter ran to Antje's farm. She was busy in the stable. He sneaked inside and filled his adored one in.

"Unfortunately I can't be with you. I have to go back to Lueneburg tomorrow. My period of apprenticeship hasn't fully run down yet.

"I'll take you".

"How would this be possible? You have to go to work tomorrow morning".

"Stuff it. Then I'll just skip work. I'll take you and that is it".

"You won't do it. Think of it, if you skip work your boss will be angry with you. And we both needn't an angry boss now".

Antje was right of course. As a leave taking wouldn't have been possible the next morning, they decided to prepone it. Manfred was not a person to be trifled with and Antje wanted to avoid a direct confrontation of the two of them by any means.

Straight eight o'clock in the morning Guenter and his father stood in front of the court building and rang the bell. Antje's custodian opened.

"What do you want here again? I won't change my mind".

"We have an appointment with Judge Jansen".

"What do you want of him"?
"We will certainly not tell you".
"He is not here".
"Yes, he is".
"How do you want to know this"?
"Because he asked us to come here".
"Well, then I am going to ask him".
"Oh, I thought he isn't here"?
The officer blushed and let the two of them pass him. Suddenly a door was pushed open.
"What are you doing here, Menke? Let the two of them enter".
"Yes, Mr. Judge. I didn't know that you made an appointment with those here".
"Those here are my guests and now see that you get back to your work. And you better don't eavesdrop any more. Then you have been officer for the longest time. Is this clear now"?
Mr. Menke only nodded subserviently and sneaked away.
"He is such a canaille! If we weren't so short of staff, I would have set him free for long. Well, anyway, come in".
While the judge took his seat behind the desk, Guenter and his father sat down in front of it.
"Now please tell me your story".

*

While Guenter filled in the judge, Mr. Menke three rooms further called the pub in Bartelshain.
"Hello, it's me".
"What do you want at this time of day"?
"Oskar you must do me a favor".
"Oh, must I"?
„Please run over to Manfred Wilbers and get him to the phone".
"Am I your leg man, Menke? Why should I do it"?
"I'll owe you something if you do it. You know it is always good to have a friend working at court. Now hurry up it is important".
"Well, all right, as an exception".
"I'll call back in ten minutes, ok"?
Ten minutes later Mr. Menke had Manfred on the line.
"What is it so urgently? You got me out of the stable".
"Guenter and his father are with Judge Jansen at the moment. I think they want to lever out my order concerning the marriage".
"Can they do this? I think you are the custody".
„Yes, but a judge always ranks above an ordinary officer. Jansen could mess up everything at once".

"That is really nasty. What are we going to do about it"?
"I can't do anything from here. I would talk to the pastor. He's your drinking mate. If he denies doing the wedding, you'll be out of it".
"That is a good idea".
After about an hour the judge was filled in.
"This Menke is crazy. What has he got against your wedding"?
"He somehow seems to be a good friend of Manfred Wilbers".
"Well, true, and he on the other side wants to avoid Antje marrying. He is frightened that you two will send him off the farm. Unfortunately there is a little problem. I allowed this guardianship personally. I didn't know anything about the backgrounds. Menke didn't tell me anyway.
Well if we want to come to a good end here, I have to talk to Antje personally. It is subscribed by law that I have to get an idea of the ward on my own before I revise something I had agreed to before, so, how do we get to your Antje"?
„I will call her and in case of emergency pick her up in Lueneburg".
„This is a good idea. As soon as you have checked this, you call me and we will make a new appointment. Towards Menke I will act the unsuspecting one. Not that he gets any bloody ideas. But one

thing I can promise you. As soon as this is over I will wipe the floor with this idiot".

Hardly back on the yard je jumped into his truck and rushed towards his job, Of course he hadn't got the whole day off and still had some tasks to do. Although being under time pressure he didn't drive to the customer straight away, but stopped at his boss's house. Je jumped out of the car and ran into the office.

"Oops, what are you doing here, shouldn't you be at Aller's already"?

"I'm already on my way, have to phone for short".

Without minding his boss's stunned face he took the receiver and dialed Lisa's number. Unfortunately Kurt was in the line and he put off without saying a word. He dialed the number of Lisa's neighbor.

"Hello, here's Guenter, would you please get Antje to the phone"?

"Dear goodness, what's the matter"?

"I'll tell you later: I have got not time, please get Antje to the phone".

"Ok, one moment please".

"Hello"?

"Hello Antje, it's me".

"Yes, what is it"?

Guenter explained her in a few words what it was about.

"Then I have to talk to Lisa first. I can't just leave here. I will call your boss when I have settled everything".

While Guenter rushed to his work and Antje filled in Lisa the phone rang on Lisa's farm. Kurt immediately took the phone.

"Hello, Kurt, it's me, Manfred".

"Nice to hear of you again, how are you"?

"Kurt, I'm sorry but I have no time. You must see to it that Antje doesn't leave your farm. Come up with something. They are hatching something".

"I will see what I can do. God knows, there's work here enough".

*

Two days later the pastor suddenly stood in the living room of Guenter's parents.

"Oops, pastor what do you want here? Did you get lost"?

"Instead of giving me a roasting you should better listen to me".

"What is it so urgently that you dare to come here"?

"We can leave out the kind words. I won't marry Antje and Guenter".

"Uh-huh and why not"?

"Because this would be against God's commandments"?

"This would be against God's commandments? What gives you that idea"?

"The woman must be subordinate to the man. Thus it is written in the bible. And a daughter must obey her father. This is written in the bible as well. If Manfred doesn't want his daughter Antje to marry, we can't do anything about it. Antje isn't fully aged yet and therefore dependent on Manfred's will. And I as the pastor can't be in violation of God's commandments, the marriage will be cancelled".

"Do you know what pastor? You can go and jump in the lake with your blathering. You have to talk big here and pretend to be holy. Isn't it true that you can be very friendly towards little girls"?

"This is a bad assumption. You can't prove anything".

"I am not going to prove something here. See that you get out of here I don't want to see types like you around here anymore. And stop your holy chatter. It makes you only sick".

"I don't know what you want. I am of a pure heart".

"Just shut up. We will work it out somehow if you like it or not".

"Do you really want to mess up with Manfred Wilbers? He will finish you if he is in rage".

"We will see. And now get lost before your holy cake hole will be damaged".

*

It should take four full months until Antje got the possibility to leave Lisa's farm at least for a few days. Kurt had done his best to keep Antje there. One day he even deliberately jumped out of a hatch to hurt his leg. It really got swollen and had put Kurt out of action for full three weeks. After that Antje wasn't able to take a leave of course.
"You know, Antje it may be that there is something going on, but whether Kurt did it deliberately or not, we cannot do without you as long as Kurt isn't able to work".
In this case not even Lisa could be persuaded. When Antje finally sat next to Guenter in the car, she felt happy for the first time in weeks. Somehow they would manage it. Furthermore she had good news for Guenter.
"Guenter"!
"Yes, what is it"?
"I think I am pregnant".
"You are pregnant"?

"Yes, our plan worked out. Now they can't prevent us from marrying".
"Well this is really good news".
"Imagine, we are going to be parents".
Judge Jansen opened the door to his office himself.
"Well Antje, tell me what's the matter with you".
Antje told for two full hours. She described the situation s on her farm into each detail. She also detailed about her great love for Guenter. She only kept silent about the sexual assaults of Manfred because she felt ashamed for herself and her mother who hadn't been able to intervene and protect her daughter. On top she was still afraid that Manfred would leave her if he knew that she hadn't been a virgin anymore.
"Well, let's see what we can do. I will demand a hearing to which I will invite you, your stepfather and your mother. If Guenter can contribute anything to finding the truth he is welcome as well. Do you agree with it"?
"Yes and what will be with the order of Mr. Menke"?
"You can forget about it. He ranges very high in my hit list anyway. If I can prove what things he really did, he will not only get rid of his job but of his pension as well. I never liked these old Nazis who walked into a readymade position after the deliberation and who allegedly had no idea what

Adolf and his companions had brought about. He will get the shock of his life anyway. But please Antje this must be kept between us, ok?"
One week later Antje Guenter Manfred and Helena gathered in the office of the judge.
"Actually this hearing should take place in the court room, but I think with us few people it will be better here".
"Well Antje state your matter here".
"I want to marry Guenter and furthermore I want that Manfred leaves my farm. He is violent, beats my mother and squanders my heritage".
Manfred was foaming with rage.
"What nonsense are you telling here? Are you out of your mind? How are you representing me? Wasn't it me who modernized the farm, who finally makes some money by delivering the Englishmen? A marriage with this good-for-nothing is out of question. He will run through the farm and we will have worked for nothing for all the years. It won't come to that".
The judge intervened.
"Mr. Wilbers did I allow you to speak"?
"No, Mr. Judge".
"Good, then stop it at once or I will continue this hearing without you. Dis you understand this, Mr. Wilbers"?
"Yes, Mr. Judge".

"See, it works. Mrs. Wilbers now to you, what do you say to Antje's statements"?

Helena starred to the floor at first and then casted frightened glances to Manfred which the judge didn't miss of course.

"Mrs. Wilbers please come outside with me. We both will have a little walk in the fresh air. You look a little pale in your face. Fresh air can do wonders".

Without caring for Manfred's angry face the judge got up tore Helena up from her chair and left the room together with her. He carefully shut the door behind him, linked Helena's arm and lead her outside to the yard.

"Well Mrs. Wilbers, are the statements of your daughter true"?

"Yes, Mr. Judge".

"Shall I have an investigation against your husband because of physical injury and compulsion"?

"No, Mr. Judge, then he will beat us to death. He several times told us that there are accidents on farms now and then. If I inform against him, one of these accidents will surely happen to us. I would think about it if you could assure me that you will imprison him and never let him out again".

"I can't do this. I must keep the laws as well. And for a life sentence it won't be enough".

"See, that is why I won't inform against him. His father had already been major under the Nazis. He arranged our marriage with his son to get my farm. I went to the Tommies. They declared they were not responsible. Such small things the Germans had to settle in between themselves. I visited even the pastor. But whoever I asked for help, nobody wanted to mess up with Adolf Wilbers and his son Alfred. The old networks are still working as you can see".

"Okay, I have to accept your opinion, although I don't approve of it. Such a man actually should be punished".

"Let it be good. Someday he will come out again and then he will kill us".

"Are you sure of it"?

"Yes I am very sure of it. and even if he doesn't do it, his father will care for it that we won't have a good life anymore".

After they had come back to the office again Guenter was also allowed to tell his story.

"Well, I have heard now all sides and I will proceed as follows. The custodianship is conveyed from Mr. Menke to me in this moment. After having carefully weighed all information and due to the fact that Antje is pregnant of Guenter…"

"What's the matter here? You piece of dirt are pregnant? Of Guenter? You can't tell me this. Have you allowed some nonentity to fuck you on the farm of the Leupert's or what"?

"Mr. Wilber, please shut your mouth at once. Otherwise I will impose a really hard fine on you. Is that clear now"?

"Yes Mr. Judge".

"As Antje is pregnant of Guenter and both of them according their age make a reasonable impression on me, I agree to the marriage".

Now to you, Guenter. What do your parents say to your intention to marry Antje"?

"They don't have anything against it. My mother says I couldn't find a better wife than Antje. This is true she is absolutely right".

„Well, then this side is clear as well. The statement of agreement must be there in written form of course. Did you understand this, Guenter"?

„Yes, I will inform my parents at once. You will have the paper on your desk tomorrow morning".

"Well, then we are ready here for now. You can go home. I will inform Mr. Menke at once.

"There is one more thing Mr. Wilbers, only that you are informed. I will keep an eye on you and your activities. Even if neither your wife nor your daughter filed a charge on you, you should control yourself in future. There is the one or other paragraph which can hurt you very much even without complaint. Furthermore according to law the farm belongs to your wife. Your wife will manage the farm. I order that Antje will inherit the

farm alone. You, Mr. Wilbers officially have neither access to the land or to the building. As I already said, there are a few laws which clearly arrange this. Did you understand this, Mr. Wilbers"?
"Yes Mr. Judge".
Manfred had obviously become pale. His flush of anger had completely gone.
Hardly arrived on the yard of the court building Manfred's rage was back again.
"This will have an aftermath, I can tell you. You won't get off like this".
He raised his hand but did not strike because he had recognized the judge who observed them though is office window.

*

Although Manfred had tried several times to torpedo the marriage of the two, the engagement was celebrated on the first Christmas Day in 1958 in the house of Guenter's parents. Manfred did not appear to underline his discontent about this marriage. Actually nobody really missed him, as they assumed after having drunk alcohol he would provoke a quarrel again. He also stayed away of the wedding which was celebrated on the last day of

January 1959 in Guenter's parental home as well. Antje and Guenter were united in happiness they had reached their aim and celebrated with their friends and relatives until the early morning.

The wedding journey had to be canceled because of lack of money. In order to allow Antje a little trip in spite, Guenter borrowed the car of his boss. They drove to Bremen, went for a long stroll through the city and allowed themselves a piece of cake and a strawberry ice cream at the banks of the Weser River.

As Uwe would take over the parental farm, Guenter moved to Antje. He even left his job to work on the farm. Unfortunately this didn't go very well from the beginning. Manfred let Guenter feel that he didn't like him, that he saw Guenter as an intruder, who had pinched his young girlfriend. Several times Manfred rudely aroused Antje and Guenter from sleep with loud noise at five in the morning.

"See that you get out of bed. Who is fucking about all night can as well get up and work the next morning".

As they both feared the outburst of the unpredictable Manfred, they joined the game for some time. After one night Manfred tanked had stood in front of their bed and threatened to gore them up at once, they both have had enough. They looked for a flat and moved out. Guenter went back to his old job and by playing music at the weekends he made some extra money to make ends meet for his small family. Dieter had been born in the meantime and needed all the attention of his mother. Antje fully merged into her mother role and lovingly cared for her offspring.

Antje had asked her mother several times to send off Manfred who still beat her. However Helena had become a broken woman in the course of the years. She didn't find the courage anymore to do something against Manfred. Helena had surrendered and vegetated more than she lived. She did all the work on the farm, had him continue to mock her and rape her. She did not live. She just functioned.

After Antje had finished her twenty first year and thus had become fully aged, she insisted on her right of inheritance. Unfortunately Manfred didn't have him displaced easily and her mother hadn't been a real help. Thus it took some month until she had fought by court that Manfred had to leave the farm. As usually Manfred raged about and put all his anger on Helena. Although she didn't have a good life at Manfred's side, she asked her daughter to allow Manfred to stay on the farm. Antje didn't agree and Manfred had to move out.

However he insisted on troubling Helena now and then. When Antje came to know about it, she confronted Manfred and told him she would publish his assaults in case he shouldn't leave her mother alone once and for all times. As his network had broken, Mr. Menke had been removed from his office and also the pastor had been pensioned off, Manfred broke down crying in the presence of Antje.

"I had had a bad childhood as well. You can't imagine how it is to grow up in the house of a madman. Do you think you were the only little girl to be due? No, my little sisters had to be available almost every day".

"But you joined the game well".

"Yes, because I had to. My father always said, see that you bring the women to heel. I didn't want it, but what should I have done? In the beginning I tried more than once to protect my sisters from my father. He beat me that much that I joined the game from this moment on".

"Stop lying. I experienced you. If you had really found it unpleasant you wouldn't have had to build up a dictatorship in our house".

"Probably I had already been shaped like this. The leopard can't change his spots after all".

"You can tell me a lot. You tortured me and my mother and raped us. I cannot remember a single day when there was peace in our house. Day and

night we were frightened of your freak-outs. So stop playing the victim".
"What can I do to prevent a publishing? Do you want any money"?
"This is a good idea. From now on you leave my mother alone and you pay me ten thousand marks".
"Ten thousand marks? Where should I take them from"?
"How much can you pay"?
"Well, three thousand at most".
"We agree on five thousand. You will give me the money tomorrow, you leave my mother alone from now on and I will be silent. If not you can already look forward to the jail. If we unpack, you are ready for a cell with grids before it".
Manfred paid and left Helena alone from now on.

*

As Guenter didn't want to work as a farmer on a small farm with hardly any profit, he continued his studies in his profession. After the technician exam he was offered a job in the central power station. Now he had regular working hours, had every weekend off and on top a salary, they could well live on. As he still was in great demand as a musician, he made some money from this side, as well. A few years later they had saved some money. This money and his part of heritage were enough to build a house in Bartelshain.

When the children were a little older, Antje qualified for auxiliary nurse. For hours she cared for people in need in the hospital or in the old people's home. Further she immediately agreed when the youth welfare service offered her the fosterage for two girls.

Carmen and Vanessa came from a family where domestic and sexual abuse had been daily fare. Antje at once took those two poor beings into her heart and lovingly cared for them. Furthermore she founded a children's play circle. Several times a week children were frolicking about the house. Antje had got two mothers enthusiastic about it and thus the house filled more and more.

After Helena had dies, Antje sold the farm. Then several inconsistencies came to light. Guenter who saw through the papers, noticed that among others the stock of trees that was noted down in the papers didn't accord to the real stock of trees. He had thoroughly checked the farm and farmland and had paced again all the fields and woods. Large areas of wood had been cut clear. Manfred and Adolf had sold the wood on the quiet without Helena, Antje or Guenter having noticed anything of it.

Antje didn't only care for the children she started to control every step. The older her own children and the foster children got, the more seldom she left the young people out of her eyes. Antje absolved an incredible amount every day. After the breakfast the children were taken to school. Then she rushed to the hospital. On her way back she did a job as domestic nurse and in the early afternoon she looked after the children of the play circle. In the evenings she regularly exhausted fell into bed. Although she often was completely worked out, she seldom could find sleep. Again and again her thoughts circled about the children and their school and play mates. Were those strange children the right, contacts for her own children? Did they really play under somebody's watch when she was not there? Didn't Dieter hurt his knee only last week? Had he possibly infected himself with it?

One evening Guenter took the word.

"Antje, it won't go on like this. You get up tired in the morning, run about the whole day and cluck on the children as if they were chickens. Our family life has completely fallen by the wayside. It is only about ill ones, old ones and children. How long do you want to go on like this? You will collapse. And what will be the use of it"?

"Guenter, we are fine. I only want to help people who didn't or don't have as much luck together as he have. The patients and the children need me. What should they do without me"?

"Antje, wake up! If you break your leg tomorrow the world won't stop to turn".

"Guenter, yu don't understand that. You grew up in happy surroundings, unfortunately I didn't. I have to take care for these people. Look, what they did to Carmen and Vanessa. They can't grow up without me".

"Yes, it is true it is hard what happens around us, but you alone can't save the world. Take it easier. Let us travel somewhere, only the two of us. I want to spend time with you and not only stumble over mountains of toys".

"You are rather selfish. The children need me don't you understand that at all"?

In the course of the years Guenter tried more than once to convince Antje of the madness of her actions but regularly only met a wall of incomprehension. He hadn't dreamed of such a life after all. Now and then he was glad to be able to leave the house. He did overwork and more and more often accepted offers for gigs. Neither during his working hours nor on weddings where he made music for dancing, they only talked about children and illnesses.

Mathilde, his sister, had married many years ago. She had got children as well, but it didn't only revolve around the little rascals. He didn't have

anything against children, but he wasn't able to bear it anymore if it only and exclusively was about children. Many years ago his brother Uwe had sold the parental farm and had migrated to America. There he has made friends with many people of German origin and built up a large circle of acquaintances.
Now and then Guenter telephoned with Uwe.
"Don't you want to come over once? There will be the Steuben parade soon. You have to see it".
Antje wasn't impressed at all.
"And what will become of the children"?
"Our children are already grown up. Even Carmen and Vanessa won't die at once, if we aren't there for two weeks. The other children will have to play somewhere else for some time".
"No way, we are doing hustle and bustle for two weeks and when we come back everything will have gone downhill".
"What should go downhill"?
"Well who knows what parties Dieter, Michaela, Carmen and Vanessa will celebrate when we are away? And who knows what kind of people they are going to bring to our house then"?
"Antje, stop it. They are not stupid. Don't you have any trust in your own children"?
"Trust is good, control is better".

"Well, then I am going to go alone. I won't turn down the invitation of my own brother. I don't see him too often after all".
"He didn't have to migrate either".
"Antje, stop it now. He did his way and it is good as it is".
Although Antje almost daily tried to talk Guenter into giving up his plan to travel to America, he didn't let her persuade himself otherwise. Only in the very last moment Antje agreed to join him. After she had decided to accompany him, she only spread hectic in the house.
"What is the matter with you? We are going to be away for only two and a half weeks".
„I have to prepare everything. You don't understand that".
While Guenter enjoyed the journey and the encounter with his brother and his wife, Antje's hectic didn't really diminish".
"What's the matter with you? Relax and enjoy our first vacancy together".
"You can talk fine. The children are playing alone at home. Doesn't that interest you at all"?
"Antje, Dieter is twenty and Michaela is eighteen. What should happen after all"?
"I don't understand you. As a mother I am worried".

„And what is the use of it? You can't change anything from here anyway".
Antje finished the discussion by demonstratively keeping silent and sitting withdrawn into herself in a corner.

*

When they returned onto German soil the children had to undergo a real inquisition.
"Mother it is enough now. You are treating us like little children"
"That's what you are after all"
"Dear goodness, wake up mother. Even if you don't want it to be true, Michaela and I are adult and Carmen and Vanessa aren't three any more as well".
"For me you will always stay my children".
After Dieter and Michaela as well as Carmen and Vanessa over the years had spread their wings and moved out, Antje more and more plunged into the caregiving. She wasn't able to bear the silence in the house and hurried from one patient to the other. Instead of allowing herself to relax, she really turned up on the contrary.

Someday there was no way forward. She had reached the end of her physical and mental power. Instead of turning a gear down she was angry about her alleged incapability. When she had reached a dead end she went to see a doctor. Some illness had to be inside her. Some illness she had to outmaneuver. She had all the examinations done. However no doctor stated any physical disorder. Several doctors advised her to take it easy and to regain her strength. She didn't allow hints of this kind to come near her. She was obsessed by helping children and ill ones.

After many an odyssey through clinics and medical offices at the end of the nineteen nineties they stated breast cancer. Finally she had a diagnosis. She had always known that something had to be within her, to hinder her from working and caring. Suddenly a wave of compassion came towards her. Finally it was her turn. Finally she got all the attendance she had always been waiting for. Now she was able to take it easier without having a bad conscience.

Operations, irradiations, chemotherapies and stays in rehabilitation clinics extended over a long time. Months became years. Sometimes she was said to be healed, then again the cancer would have spread. Guenter still stuck with her, gave her security and visited her as often as he as his schedule allowed it.

No way was too long for him, no hindrance too big to prevent him visiting Antje.

Now they finally had time for each other. Now they had talks long overdue. Now Antje was thrown to herself. Now she couldn't but thoroughly deal with herself and her life. Only now she found the courage to enlighten Guenter about all the events in her life and leave him to read the diaries she had secretly written. Now insights rose inside her she had never thought to be possible. Now she realized what she had expected of Guenter and her children to put up with, just to be praised by other people.

Guenter had rarely been able to comprehend the activities of his wife, her craving for appreciation. But he had never ceased to love her. After many hours together, after many intensive talks Antje died in his arms.

*

Guenter gave me extracts of her diaries and had several talks with me. Sometimes he was sad. Sometimes he smilingly told me about a little girl who had golden straw in her hair when she frolicked about a harvested corn field or rolled down a meadow.

*

Dear reader!
Now you got to know my life. I still remember almost every incident as if it had happened yesterday. I sit on the knees of my father or on the lap of my grandmother.
Sometimes I frolic about a harvested corn field with Guenter and his brothers and sisters. Afterwards my mother looks at me censoriously, because I again have golden straw in my curly hair. Smilingly she looks for the haulms and tears them off. Then again we roll down a meadow. My dress is fully green afterwards, but we have rally fun doing it.
I watch my grandmother milking. Of course she gives me a glass of the still warm milk. In summer we rollick around in the fields. In fall we sit at the potato fire and hold spitted potatoes into the fire. In winter we love to slide over frozen puddles. If it rains we go to the attic to let us fall from the roof bean into the soft hay. Utterly fearlessly we flung ourselves into the depth of two or three meters to land softly.
Unfortunately some unfriendly people cared that my idyll got ricky-tick chapped. I was suddenly thrown into a world I hadn't known before. The dear God later gave me the dear Guenter to my

side. Of course it had been a learning process for him as well and I think it wasn't always easy with me. But I think he really loves me. Who else would have done so much for me?

I only shortly told him about the sexual assaults on me. I had been silent about this side of my life until now. In the beginning I had been frightened that he would not love me and marry me if he got to know that I hadn't been a virgin anymore. Later I shoveled myself up with work so that many things were forgotten. I didn't want to lose him. I wanted him to love me. I wanted a good life at his side. it wasn't always been easy for him with me. Often I crossed his plans and put myself into the center. I hope he will keep me in good memory.

Now that you, dear reader red these lines, I am not among you anymore. I asked Guenter to publish my records to show that it is not good to put up with everything, to show that the so-called idyll of the village often exists only in phantasy. In the course of my life I spoke to people of different regions. There are obviously similar procedures in every village, good and bad people.

Sometimes you simply have to be courageous, try something completely new. Leave behind the convenience which had been paid by much unpleasant, to finally become happy. I wrote these reports for myself. I wanted to remember. I wanted my life to be a reminder as well. It is not bad if you don't learn from the mistakes of others, but you don't have to make every mistake yourself.

I devote these records to my dear husband Guenter, to my son Dieter and my daughter Michaels, who enriched my life and in hard hours lifted me up again and again. Besides I don't want to forget my foster daughters Carmen and Vanessa, who often troubled me much, but on the other hand cheered me up again and again and who painfully made me realize from time to time that you mustn't cage up children who are spreading their wings.

During the last months I had much time to think. I realized a few things which I if I consider it properly, had pushed to the back of my mind for almost my life time. I haven't always acted honestly. Dieter was created to give our marriage a reason and Michaela, because I thought it would be proper to have two children. Furthermore I had got much attention during my first pregnancy. This attention I wanted to experience a second time.

Furthermore I didn't only help unselfishly. Now and then I made myself indispensable to get consideration, to be praised. I used my foster daughters as well as the children of the play circle to fill the emptiness in my life, to be in service round the clock in order not to have to think and not to tear up old wounds.

However I had been clearly taught that you cannot run away from your past after all. Sometimes it was fine for a few days or even a few weeks. But then the pictures were there again and more than once I woke up in sweat because I thought I would be on Manfred's lap.

I hope that you, my children are able to forgive me. I really loved you all from the depth of my heart. When I often controlled you round the clock, then it was because I wanted to spare you a life as I had to live. I wanted to protect you, wanted to prevent meeting people who were the wrong ones in my eyes and that you maybe got to the bad.

Also Uwe, Mathilde, Jochen, Lisa Leupert and all the others should not be unmentioned. They accompanied and supported me in my childhood and many of them for all my lifetime. Without the help of Jochen, Guenter and I probably hadn't been able to marry at all. And Judge Jansen showed me that there are also good people.

Now my life has almost finished and sometimes I am a bit sad. But the world will turn on after me. Children will be born and old and sick people will die. I experienced and saw a lot. Now it is enough.

Dagmar Hildebrandt

Strong-Lady-Books

Elisabeth Margaretha Countess of Schoengau-Brixendorf
Sara, the Weasel

Viktoria Grantz
My father, the diacon
The sold countess

Simone Petzold
Sweet fall of life

Lena Birkthal
Life in the matriarchy

Viktoria Grantz
Die verkaufte Gräfin
Das Ende des Jägers
Denn sie schenkten mir ein zweites Leben
Vera, die Moorfrau
In 80 Jahren rund um Hörnde
Die Prinzessin vom Leuchtturm
Mein Vater, der Diakon

Simone Petzold
Das bunte Leben der Renata Komanetschy
Die Wende meines Lebens
Mein weiter Blick aufs Meer
Der süße Herbst des Lebens

Lena Birkthal
Leben im Matriarchat

Michaela Main
Von Frau zu Frau – nicht alltägliche Gesundheitstipps

Michaela Holst
Landfrauen

Katja Groening
Die Burg der Nymphen

Eva Maria Thalbach
Das Ende des Dornenwaldes

Yvonne Zündler
Mitten im Abschaum
Die Stille eines Lebens

Heide Marie Zimmer
Das Mädchen Yvonne
Flucht und Heimkehr
Die Goldesel-Töchter

Elisabeth Margaretha Gräfin von Schöngau-Brixendorf
Sara, das Wiesel
Goldenes Stroh in meinem Haar

www.starke-frauen.org